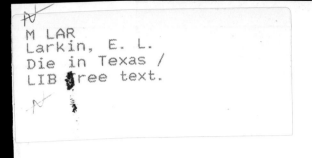

DIE IN TEXAS

DIE IN TEXAS

•

E.L. Larkin

AVALON BOOKS
NEW YORK

PRINTED IN THE UNITED STATES OF AMERICA
ON ACID-FREE PAPER
BY HADDON CRAFTSMEN, BLOOMSBURG, PENNSYLVANIA

In fond memory of my husband,
James H. Larkin

Chapter One

There are a lot of miles between Corpus Christi and the New Mexico line; long, hot, gritty miles. Red Texas dust had turned my old blue Corona a dirty ocher color, my tank top was streaked with sweat, and my hair looked like a Brillo pad.

I greeted the welcoming *New Mexico: Land of Enchantment* sign with a sour grimace.

"The Pacific Northwest may not be perfect, but it sure as sin beats this combination of heat and mesquite," I told myself, scowling at my reflection in the mirror.

According to my old friend and schoolmate, Katy Valentine, October was the nicest month of the year in this part of the country. Maybe she thought so, but as far as I was concerned the last ten days had been anything but nice. It was certainly October, but I hadn't seen a day below ninety, the scenery was monotonous, and the bugs were eating me up alive.

I own and operate a small genealogy/research business, Confidential Research Inc., in Seattle, Washington, where anything over seventy-five degrees is considered very hot weather. Most of my work is done by telephone or computer, but three weeks ago I had agreed to do some research in south Texas that I had to take care of in person. The inquiry had not turned out well, and ninety is too blamed hot.

Truthfully, however, my main reason for taking the job had been to see Katy, and if I read her map correctly I would be doing so within minutes.

Katy and I have been friends since childhood. We were born a few weeks apart thirty some years ago, lived next door to each other, and grew up sharing everything, including early boyfriends. I hadn't seen her since her marriage to Billy Joe Valentine two years ago. We do still write or phone at least once a month, but things are not quite the same. She's married, I'm not. I work, she doesn't. And Del Rio, New Mexico, is a long way from Seattle.

Katy's last letter contained the map I was looking at, drawn in her usual slapdash way on the back of an old plumbing bill. On it, scrawled above a crossroad symbol, she had written *5 mi* and doodled a stick drawing of what I took to be the Valentine ranch house.

I was a scant five miles past the state line when I spotted the crossroad, a rough single-lane track surfaced with pea gravel and potholes. Clouds of glittering dust trailed in my wake as, after about a half mile, the road came to an abrupt end in front of a huge mound of sand. To my left, behind a barb wire fence, several trucks emblazoned with the yellow and black New Mexico state emblem were parked beside a shed. The gate to the enclosure sported a padlock and large KEEP OUT sign.

Definitely not the road to Katy's.

There wasn't enough room on the road itself to turn around, but on my right a narrow alleyway between the sand pile and a stack of railroad ties looked as if it led to a more open space. I could see the edge of a metal building over the sand. I shifted into low and started to turn.

A second later, three men careened around the end of the ties—straight into my path.

Terrified, I stood on the brakes. I was barely moving, but I came close to crashing into all three of them. I started to yell, to ask what the heck did they think they were playing at, but before I could get the words out I realized they weren't *playing* at anything. They were fighting, and one man was swinging some kind of club. If they noticed how close I came to hitting them it didn't slow them up any. They went right on hitting each other.

I've been accused of having a feisty disposition, but I'm actually a devout coward. Just the thought of getting mixed up in any kind of a fight was enough to scare me. I slammed the Corona into reverse and went roaring back to the highway before the dust of my arrival had a chance to settle. Within yards the indistinct figures of the three men behind me disappeared into the glittering haze. I hoped I was equally invisible. Unfortunately, by the time my knees quit shaking I was far down the highway and had no idea where I was in relation to Katy's map.

As it happened, the town of Del Rio was less than a mile farther on. The first thing I saw was a car wash and gas station with a public telephone at the corner of the building. The attendant, a teenage boy, took care of the car while I phoned Katy.

Twenty minutes later I came to a stop in front of a sprawling two-story frame house that Katy had described as a ten-room treasure trove.

"Demary! Oh, Demary." Katy came flying down the porch steps as I shut off the motor and got out. "I am so glad to see you. So glad!"

Her welcoming hug nearly knocked me over.

"Hey, take it easy," I protested, laughing. "You're about to strangle me."

"I'm just so darn happy to see you." She stood back to smile, then wrapped her arms around me again. There were tears in her eyes.

Her welcome should have warned me that all wasn't as rosy as her letters had made out, but I was glad to see her too and chalked the tears up to her volatile personality.

Katy is tall and slender, with silky dark blond hair and brilliant green eyes. A spectacular combination. I've envied her looks and figure ever since I can remember. I'm a very unspectacular five-foot-two, at least ten pounds overweight, and have the garden-variety blue eyes. I do have naturally curly auburn hair, but it is beginning to need help.

Once past the emotions of reunion we spent the rest of the afternoon chattering like teenagers, catching up on what we had been doing since our last letters. We managed to talk our way through my shower, a change of clothes, several glasses of iced tea, and were still finding plenty to say when Katy took me for a tour of the house, barns, and stables.

The house was crammed with antebellum furniture that made me drool, including a solid black walnut armoire in one of the bedrooms that I almost cried over. All the bedrooms contained at least one rack draped with a magnificent hand-pieced quilt.

"The ranch has been in Billy Joe's family for over a hundred years," Katy told me. "His great-grandfather homesteaded here the same year General Mackenzie's Fourth Cavalry defeated the combined tribes at Palo Duro Canyon in 1874."

"Not the same house, surely?" I didn't recognize the architectural style but it didn't look all that old.

"Of course not, silly. This one was built in 1930. It's a typical West Texas ranch house. Billy Joe inherited the place from his grandfather when he was just a kid. Both his parents were killed during the Vietnam War. His father in Nam, his mother in a car accident."

"West Texas? I thought we were in New Mexico."

"The ranch is twenty-seven hundred acres in all, and although the house is on the New Mexico side of the line, most of the land is in Texas. The state line runs through the property just east of that barn." Katy pointed.

"How strange."

"What?"

"The property being in two states."

"Not really. Quite a few ranches cross the line. The King ranch, for instance, covers miles of both states. Two of

Leroy's sections cross. One of his sections runs almost to the Mexican border on the Texas side."

"Leroy?"

"Leroy Scarber. One of our friends. You'll meet him."

I had never met Billy Joe either and was looking forward to doing so. He and Katy had met in Houston two years ago while she was there visiting an aunt and were married six weeks later in a Texas wedding spectacular that included five hundred guests and a barbeque. I was supposed to have been Katy's maid of honor, but had been in an accident the day before I was scheduled to leave home. I was still in the hospital when they left on their honeymoon.

"Billy Joe is really anxious to see you," Katy told me. "He called early this afternoon to see if you were here yet and said he'd made reservations at the country club. We'll go on out there as soon as we're ready. He'll join us when he gets in. The airport, such as it is, is just down the road from the club."

"Gets in? Where is he?"

"I'm not sure. Lubbock, maybe. He sent a couple hundred head over there to be auctioned. I think he and Leroy took Leroy's plane, though, so they could be just about anywhere," Katy said, shrugging. She finished off the rest of the drink she was carrying around and stood up to go.

I glanced at my watch. It was six o'clock and already dark. When the sun went down in the plains country it didn't fool around. It fell right off the end of the world. Night came in a hurry.

Chapter Two

The Del Rio Country Club was a surprise. I don't know what I expected, but it certainly wasn't the elegant establishment we entered after an attendant had whisked Katy's Mercedes away from the door.

A huge place with strong overtones of *Gone With The Wind* and an abundance of semi-tropical greenery in mammoth planters, it was so new that parts of the building weren't yet completed. We passed several unfinished rooms as Katy showed me around. The pro shop was still only half painted and scaffolding lined the hall to the exercise rooms.

"Do you like it?" Katy asked. "Billy Joe and I helped design and furnish it. He's chairman of the building committee. The old building burned down in January."

"It's beautiful. Very nice. But how ... I mean, Del Rio

E.L. Larkin

is such a small town. How could the members afford to build a place like this?"

"Lots of insurance. And this isn't one of those snooty exclusive places, so we have loads of members. Anyone can join. Just step into the office and pay the entrance fee. Which isn't too high either. One of our best golfers is the night fry cook at a fast food place in town. A lot of people join just so their kids can use the swimming pool. And Del Rio is an oil town anyway."

"So?" I had seen dozens of oil well pump-jacks on my way into town but this was still an expensive facility for a community the size of Del Rio.

"Oil is still black gold. Where do you think Billy Joe got all his money? Not just from cattle, believe me."

"I thought the price of oil had dropped some."

"Oh, it did, but it shot right back up. It's holding steady now. Investors in newer wells are feeling the pinch of the high cost of drilling, but there aren't that many new wells around Del Rio. This is an old town with old fields. Most of the wells on Billy Joe's land were drilled in the thirties and have been producing steadily every since. We're right in the middle of the biggest pool of oil in the country. It costs to service them, of course, but that's nothing compared to the cost of putting down a new well."

We moved on into the bar. I gazed around at the decor while Katy ordered the drinks.

"What caused the fire in the old clubhouse?" I asked.

Katy shook her head. "I don't know. I was in Houston visiting Aunt Pastene. I think Billy Joe said something about faulty wiring, but I'm not sure. Nobody got hurt, thank goodness. The fire started about four in the morning after everyone had left. No one was too sorry it burned, though. The old place had all the comforts of a barn. Actually, part of the place *had* been a barn. Some old rancher donated the land, a hundred and fifty acres, with barn, to build a club. Back in the fifties."

"This is sure no barn," I said. The room was as dark as a tomb, but what I could see of it was done in a Victorian style with a lot of red plush and gilt. "The mirrors alone must have cost a small fortune."

"Aren't they gorgeous? I ordered them from France."

"And they did cost a fortune," a male voice said.

"Billy Joe." Katy turned so quickly she nearly spilled her drink. "Don't sneak up on me like that! You scared the tar out of me."

"Sorry, honey. I surely didn't mean to." Billy Joe gave us a wide, white-toothed smile. "And this little Kewpie doll must be Demary Jones."

I held out my hand. "Give that man a big seegar," I cooed. I can be just as insincere as the next guy.

"Yes, of course it's Demary," Katy said in an cranky tone. "Demary, this is Billy Joe."

He drawled something about waiting so long to meet me and took my hand with a sweeping, courtly gesture that made me want to snatch it back out of his grasp. If he'd been anybody but Katy's husband I would have taken an instant dislike to him. Southern charm raises the hair on the back of my neck. The last man who had "charmed" me with a Texas drawl ended up trying to kill me.

"Where have you been, Billy Joe?" Katy asked. "It's after seven and we're starved."

"I'm sorry, honey. Leroy's plane took a coughing spell and we had to set down on an access road over by Seminole. We just got back. That's why I look like this." He slapped dust from his dark pants. His shirt, a pristine sparkling white, was open at the top to show his sun-bronzed neck. "I knew you'd be waitin' on me so I didn't go home to change."

He signaled the barman, who brought him a tall glass of what looked like straight bourbon over ice.

"What was wrong with the plane?" Katy asked.

"No idea, honey. Leroy got it going again, though, so it was all right."

Billy Joe's oh-so-casual attitude struck me as being a little overdone. Having to make a forced landing couldn't have been all that much fun. I said as much.

"You're right about that," Billy Joe agreed. "Leroy thinks that lil' bird of his is the next best thing to walking on water but I favor a pickup. May take a little longer to get there but at least if it quits on me I can get out and walk."

Later, in the dining room, I got a better look at him. My first horrified thought was that he was one of the men I'd seen fighting, then I realized he couldn't have been. The landing had simply been a lot more serious than he wanted Katy to know. His brown eyes looked feverish, his right hand was skinned, and he had trouble using his left arm.

His overall appearance was something of a surprise. I'd seen many pictures of him—at least two dozen of the wedding alone—and none had given me a real sense of what he was like. Very attractive without being actually handsome, he was big-boned, with wide shoulders and a deep chest—both of which had showed even in his wedding tux—but I hadn't had a mental picture of his height. I had imagined him well over six feet, while he was actually about five-eleven. The pictures hadn't hinted at his overwhelming personality either. Even when silent he dominated the table, exuding power and authority in a suave, easy manner that allowed no opposition.

He ordered for both Katy and me, without consulting Katy and only asking me how I liked my steak done. All of this irritated me, but he did it so smoothly I couldn't protest without sounding like a jerk.

The dinner, a seafood cocktail with enormous gulf shrimp, a two-inch-thick steak done to perfection, and tiny new potatoes with a butter and parsley glaze, was exceptionally good. I could have made a meal of just the Caesar salad.

A number of people stopped by the table to be introduced while we were eating. They seemed to know a lot more about me than I learned about them. Katy must have been doing a lot of talking before I arrived. Not that I minded—they were all welcoming—but some of them had such pronounced accents I had a hard time understanding what they were saying.

We were finishing up with coffee strong enough to take the glaze off the cup when the law arrived. He appeared to be in his late fifties and reminded me of Jimmy Stewart. Tall, about six-four, and thin, he looked as if he had just stepped out of a B-grade western movie, complete with star. The huge gun on his hip was sheathed in a tooled leather holster adorned with silver conchos, and his creamy white ten-gallon hat made him look even taller.

I couldn't help gawking, particularly when he swept off his hat and greeted us with, "Howdy, folks."

Billy Joe introduced him as Sheriff Orin Cato.

Cato inclined his head, said how nice it was to meet me, spoke to Katy in a slow, courteous voice, and then told Billy Joe he'd like to speak to him privately.

Billy Joe hesitated.

"Maybe we could step outside," the sheriff said softly.

"No sense in that," Billy Joe said. "Demary here is practically one of the family. What's the problem, Orin? Don't tell me you're having trouble with rustlers again."

The last remark, accompanied by a wink in my direction, didn't amuse Sheriff Cato. His expression hardened.

"No, Billy Joe, I just thought you ought to know one of your hands was found a bit ago. Dead."

"Dead?" Billy Joe snapped to attention. "What happened to him? Get in a wreck?"

"Looks like he got in a brawl that turned serious. Maybe more so than anyone intended."

"A fight? None of my men . . ." Billy Joe frowned. "Who was it?"

"McCall. Gary McCall."

During the general consternation generated by the sheriff's remarks I happened to glance at Katy. The expression on her face made me wonder if Gary McCall was more to her than just one of her husband's hired hands.

Chapter Three

Katy's reaction to the sheriff's announcement bothered me but I didn't have time to think about it. I was too concerned with controlling my own expression as the two men went on talking.

"Gary? Are you sure?" Billy Joe asked in a shocked voice. "It's not like him . . ."

"Calvin Black identified him," the sheriff interrupted. "Says he'd seen him out at your place. Although I'd like you to take a look tomorrow just to be sure. His body is in the hospital morgue."

Billy Joe nodded. "Yeah, okay. I'll go over there." He frowned. "It doesn't sound like Gary. Fighting, I mean. He was kind of a quiet guy. Where . . . ?"

"A couple of kids found him in the state sand and gravel yard south of town. Off Highway Eighteen."

Something caught the sheriff's attention on the other side

of the room. His eyes narrowed, giving his face a look of malevolence that startled me. The expression was gone when he refocused his attention on Billy Joe, making me wonder if I'd really seen it.

"The kids were dirt-biking," he went on, "and I guess they nearly ran over him. Shook 'em up some. They came high-tailing it back into Calvin's and he eventually notified me. It's my jurisdiction."

"When? When did all this happen?"

"Can't say for sure yet. Sometime this afternoon. The foreman of the road crew says he was out there at noon to check on some equipment. He wasn't over where the body was found, but he thinks he would have seen it if it had been there then."

"No. I mean when did the kids find him?"

The sheriff took a notecard out of his shirt pocket and looked at it. "I haven't talked to Calvin yet so I'm not certain. My office took the call at four-fifteen. The kids must have found him shortly before that."

"Uh, excuse me," I broke in. "I was . . . uh . . . I mean, I came in on Highway Eighteen this afternoon. Was the body right on the highway?" It was a stupid question, but the best I could come up with when I changed my mind mid-sentence and decided not to let the whole dining room know I had possibly seen the killing.

The sheriff answered gravely. "No, ma'am. He was found some distance from the highway."

As he and Billy went on talking I took a quick look at Katy. She was watching them with a mildly shocked expression that seemed almost normal. For a second I wondered if I'd been mistaken before, but her fingers, twisting her napkin into a rope under the table, betrayed her. She caught the direction of my gaze and dropped the napkin into her lap.

Katy had never been promiscuous. However, a lot could have happened since I'd seen her last. She may have changed more than I knew. She and Billy Joe had been married less than two years, though, and I couldn't quite picture her having an affair with a ranch hand anyway. Especially not with the kind I'd seen working around the place that afternoon. Not that they weren't nice enough men. They were just too . . . picturesque.

Up to her marriage, Katy had dated no one but Madison Avenue executive types. And while Billy Joe didn't exactly fall into that category, he was no rough-cut cowboy either.

I had quit listening to the men, and was trying to decide how to tell the sheriff I'd seen the fight, when he left rather abruptly. Billy Joe got up and followed him a moment later. I thought of waiting until morning. I could always say I hadn't realized I knew anything significant until after he was gone, but decided it was better to get it over with. Actually, I hadn't seen anything significant. In fact, I hadn't seen much of anything at all. I'd been too spooked, but I could narrow the time down. And I could tell him how many men were involved even if I couldn't identify them.

Katy had turned and was talking to the people at the table behind us, so I got up and followed the two men into the foyer. Although they couldn't have been more than a minute ahead of me, neither of them was anywhere in sight. Nor were they in the bar, which was totally empty. I knew they couldn't have gone far, so I trotted back across the foyer to the hall on the far side leading to the exercise and locker rooms.

It too was empty, but as I turned back I heard a door open somewhere behind me and an angry male voice say, "Find out who was in that car! Whoever it was saw all three of us, and could have seen the bird."

The speaker's accent made it hard for me to understand the words. A second man made a remark I didn't catch at all.

"Maybe, maybe not. You want to take that chance?" the first one replied.

One of them said something about a license number, and then the first voice said, "No, but at least I did see it was an old Toyota. Tan color. There can't be that many of them around. Get some men out looking for the thing."

My heart did a half-gainer. If the speaker wasn't one of Gary's killers I'd be almighty surprised. Thank goodness for the Texas dust that had turned my poor old blue Corona a dirty tan. And they apparently hadn't noticed that my car had a Washington plate, not New Mexico. Possibly because my front end plate was old and rusty. New plates were due to come out next year.

I thought of going back and trying to find Billy Joe, but discarded the idea immediately. I needed to get a look at these two first, and without either of them seeing me.

When one of them spoke again I slid around the corner and into the shadow of a six-foot dieffenbachia in a brass planter. The men were across from me, about thirty feet down the hall at the far end of a line of scaffolding. They were partly hidden by a canvas drop-cloth draped over the side of a tall ladder. The man facing me was dressed much like Billy Joe in dark pants, a white dress shirt, and a string tie with a turquoise slide. I couldn't see his face. The other man had his back to me but I recognized him immediately. Even with the dim lighting, there was no mistaking the tall, lanky figure topped by the big cream-colored hat. Unless my eyes had suddenly gone bad on me, the second man was Sheriff Orin Cato.

Chapter Four

Still in a mild state of shock, I made it back to the dining room without seeing anyone, or anyone seeing me, as far as I could tell. Learning that the fight I'd seen resulted in someone's death hadn't been a pleasant addition to dinner to start with, and identifying Sheriff Cato as one of those responsible didn't improve the situation any. Truthfully, it scared the stuffing out of me. This would make the second time I'd been mixed up in a murder involving a lawman. And I did believe it was a murder, not an accident. Two against one is no mishap, especially when the one ends up dead. It could be manslaughter, but it was no accident. I had no idea what to do next and was beginning to wish I'd never left Seattle.

I do operate an investigative agency, and I have gotten myself involved in a couple of murder investigations, but not on purpose. The bulk of my business is historical research and genealogy, and although I do some work for law firms and insurance agencies they don't commit too many homicides. I don't take criminal cases, and I didn't want anything to do with this one.

I went to work for George Crane at Confidential Research and Inquiry straight out of college, when it was a detective agency. I think I had some idea that working for a detective agency was glamorous. George disabused me of that notion in short order. I started out as a general dogsbody, doing all the boring stuff like filing and making out the bills. George did insist I get a PI license, however, and he taught me what little I know about the business. I turned out to be good at some of the work. I'm a natural-born snoop. Then George was killed in a senseless drive-by shooting and I inherited CRI by default. George had no relatives. I incorporated the business, dropped the "Inquiry," and in time turned it into what I do best. Research and genealogy.

When I got back to the table, Billy Joe and Katy were talking to an attractive woman with a deep tan and a charming smile. Her sun-streaked brown hair was cut in a wedge that framed her face in a soft natural curve. They were discussing an upcoming bridge tournament when I sat back down. Katy introduced the woman as one of her best friends, Linda Cameron.

"Do you play bridge, Demary?" Linda asked.

"No. Not at all."

"That's too bad. We'd love to have you play with us next week," she said. She talked faster than anyone else I'd spoken with, but for some reason she was easier to understand. "We're having an all women's tournament here at the club. No men allowed at all. Why don't you come anyway? We'll teach you how to play."

I made some kind of noncommittal comment and shot Katy a look of warning. I'd spent my entire four years of college refusing to learn that dismal game and I wasn't about to be caught now.

"Linda's a shark. She loves to take the sucker's money," Katy said, smirking at me from behind her napkin.

I didn't rise to the bait. Linda did.

"I do not! Katy! What a thing to say." She waved her hands as if she were being attacked by a swarm of bees and turned back to me. "You have such an unusual name, Demary. Is it an old family name?"

"Actually, yes. It was my Scottish grandfather's name. He pronounced it Dem-ry, though. I pronounce it De-mary."

After a few more pleasantries Linda left us and another couple came over. I never did catch their names, and, of course, couldn't understand half of what either of them said. Apparently they had been at the airport when Billy Joe and Leroy left in what the man called "Leroy's flyin' wreck." Billy Joe took the razzing with easy good nature. The pair finally pulled up chairs and Billy Joe ordered a round of after-dinner drinks that tasted like mouthwash, but I was so preoccupied I drank mine without thinking.

Between trying to carry on a polite conversation when I wasn't sure what the other people were saying, and trying to make up my mind what to do, I was getting antsy. I knew I should report to someone what little I knew about

Gary McCall's death but I felt so out of place, so disoriented, I couldn't think how to go about doing it. There were bound to be other men in Sheriff Cato's office, but I didn't know who they were, nor how to contact them without alerting the sheriff.

I also found it strange that no one said anything more about the dead man. Normally, at least within my circle of acquaintances, people tend to talk of nothing else when someone they know is killed, by accident or otherwise, but neither Billy Joe nor Katy referred to Gary again. I wanted someone to at least mention him because I had a few questions. Actually, I had a whole lot of questions, but I didn't want to call attention to my interest by asking them unless someone else brought up the subject.

I thought I might have an opportunity to ask something when another tall lawman came by the table and was introduced as Calvin Black, Del Rio Chief of Police. The chief was a good-looking guy with a bandito mustache, straight dark hair, and a big smile. His hand-tailored uniform fit like he'd been shoe-horned into it. He took my hand, murmuring my name in that up-close personal way some men think is sexy. I always wonder if they think I need a hearing aid.

He didn't refer to Gary and left within a few minutes, to Katy's evident relief. She'd hardly spoken to him. In fact, she was almost rude. I wondered why. He certainly seemed pleasant enough, despite obviously thinking of himself as a stud.

He was followed by a tall, elegant man with white hair and a definite Boston accent. Billy Joe introduced him as

Arnold Johnson, his lawyer. Mr Johnson excused himself for interrupting our dinner and held an odd, stilted conversation with Billy Joe for a few minutes. Then he told me he was delighted to have met me and left, leaving me with the distinct impression that something was going on beneath the smooth surface of his remarks.

Earlier, during dinner, Billy Joe had decided I was going to go home in his car. He announced his decision again as we were leaving, claiming it would give us a chance to get acquainted on our own. I was quick to agree. It would give me a chance to tell him about the sheriff.

We were waiting for the two cars to be brought around when one of the women I'd been introduced to at dinner, Joleen, came down the steps and stopped beside us.

"Katy, wasn't it one of your hands that was killed this afternoon?" she asked. "Didn't I see you with him out to the Texas Bar?"

Katy never missed a beat. "The Texas Bar? That dingy place out on the highway by the auction barns? What in the world were you doing in there, Joleen?"

"I wasn't," Joleen snapped, caught off guard. "I mean . . . uh . . . I was driving by and thought I saw you going in."

"Hardly," Katy said, giving the other woman her classiest look of distaste. "I don't patronize that kind of place."

She handed the parking valet a folded bill and got into her car.

Joleen turned back and said something to Billy Joe that I couldn't translate.

Whatever it was, he didn't respond. He helped me into

the passenger seat of his car, went around to the driver's side, and we were on our way.

We weren't far from the country club grounds when Billy Joe took hold of the conversation, and try as I did I couldn't bring it around to Gary McCall or Sheriff Cato. With someone else I might have simply told him to put a sock in it, but I didn't know him that well. It's a little difficult interrupting the conversation of a more-or-less stranger to tell him you not only think you witnessed a murder, but that the local sheriff is one of the bad guys. As a result, when the short ride was over and we pulled up in front of the house, I knew more about ranching than I had before. I also knew more about Billy Joe Valentine than I think he intended. I'm a good listener when I want to be.

He handed me out of the car in front of the house in his courtly manner, but surprisingly left me to find my way to the door by myself. Not that it was dark. All the lights along the front of the house were on. I picked up a small leather folder someone had dropped on the walk and waited on the steps for him to return from parking his car.

One thing I had learned on the ride home was that he and Sheriff Orin Cato went back a long way. They had both grown up here in Del Rio, and although I didn't get the impression they were bosom buddies, it sounded as if they were too close for me to accuse the sheriff of being involved in Gary's death. At least not without hard proof.

Chapter Five

I woke up at 5:15 the next morning to the sounds of a marital dispute—Katy's half of it anyway. Katy's father and two brothers were deep-sea fishermen. She'd spent a lot of time around the Ballard docks when she was growing up and learned some pretty salty language. When she's angry enough she uses it, loud and strong. I couldn't hear Billy Joe, but from the tone of Katy's voice, which I certainly could hear, he was holding his own. The verbal battle ended with the slam of what I took to be their bedroom door, footsteps going downstairs, and the firm closure of the outside door. In a few minutes I heard a car start and drive away. There were a few banging sounds from down the hall, then it was quiet again.

I thought about going to check on Katy but she knew where I was. If she wanted me she could yell; we were only two doors apart. I went back to sleep.

I woke the second time with the sun streaming in my window and Katy hammering on my door.

"Wake up in there," she called. "Are you dead, or what?"

"No, but you will be if you don't have a cup of coffee in your hand," I yelled back as I sat up and pushed my hair out of my eyes. Katy came in with two mugs and a thermo-pitcher full of steaming brew that smelled wonderful.

"You're as mean as ever in the morning," she said, handing me a brimming mug. "No wonder you're afraid to marry Sam. One taste of your less-than-sunny morning disposition and he'd file for divorce." She was referring to my long-time friend, and once fiancé, Sam Morgan, a detective lieutenant with the Seattle police.

"Look who's talking. If this morning is any example, it's a wonder Billy Joe hasn't dumped you long since," I said, taking a scalding sip.

She scowled. "What's more likely is that I'll end up shooting the s.o.b. some day. That story about him and Leroy having plane trouble was bull. They were off chasing women, that's where they were. Look at his hand, he was in a bar fight somewhere, sure as heck."

I didn't like to admit it—even to myself—but I *had* wondered about his hand.

"What makes you think it's a woman?" I asked. "He could have—"

"Because he's been seeing other women since the day we got married," she interrupted, her voice harsh with jealousy. "I think he was playing around the week after we got home from our honeymoon, I was just too dumb to realize it at the time."

"Why do you stay married to him then?" I knew I wouldn't under those conditions, and putting up with that kind of thing wasn't like Katy either. At least not the Katy I had always known.

She shrugged, suddenly looking drained and tired, her anger gone. "I don't know why I stay. Maybe because I love him. I like the kind of life we live. Billy Joe has one sugar pot of a lot more money than I realized when I married him, and I like being able to fly to Dallas any time I feel like going shopping at Neiman Marcus, or doing anything else I want to do."

That didn't sound like Katy either. "You were making good money before you married him," I reminded her. "What makes you so sure he's fooling around, Katy? Have you actually caught him with anyone?"

"No, of course not. If I ever caught him . . . no, I've never seen him with anyone, but half the time I don't know where he is."

That sounded to me like plain ol' jealousy. I pushed myself into a more comfortable position against the pillows and held out my mug for a refill. "From what you say, this is a big ranch. It must take days just to ride around all of it."

Katy filled both our mugs, then wandered over to the window to stare out at the barns and corrals. My room faced east, toward the Texas line.

"You've been watching too many old John Wayne movies," she said finally, coming back to sit on the end of the bed. "If he wanted to check fences he'd drive or fly. And anyway, that isn't what I mean. He isn't just gone all afternoon, sometimes he's gone for days, and when I ask him where he's been he always has some smooth story I can't check on."

"I don't understand. You mean he just goes out in the morning and doesn't come back for days? He doesn't tell you he's going to be gone? Doesn't call?"

"No, not like that. Take today. He said he was going over to Lubbock this afternoon and didn't know when he'd be back. That's what we were fighting about. You're here so he probably will be back, but otherwise he might call this evening and say he'd met some ol' boy he knows from Johnson City or someplace, and that they were going down to his spread to see a prize bull and he'd be home Saturday. Or maybe that he and ol' so-and-so were going to fly to Dallas to an auction. Whatever, and then I don't see him for a couple of days."

"Well, maybe . . ."

"Yes, maybe it's the truth. I know a lot of other women around here complain about the same thing so it isn't even unusual. And lots of times it's true, but somehow, lately, I just don't believe him . . . he's doing something else and I know it."

"It doesn't have to be a woman."

"Not necessarily, but knowing Billy Joe, a woman is most likely. And if I ever catch the sorry son I'll kill him," Katy said, laughing now. "But not today."

She poured the last of the coffee into our mugs.

"And what if he catches you?"

Katy made a sour face. "You pick up on things too fast, Demary."

"Maybe I just know you too well. But what about it? How well did you know Gary McCall?" I asked, putting my mug aside.

"Not as well as you're probably thinking. He'd only been working here a couple of months. I do feel bad about him getting killed though. He didn't seem like the type to get into any kind of a brawl."

I wanted to tell her about seeing the fight but decided not to. It wasn't that I didn't trust her, I just wasn't sure how she really felt about Gary. There was something in her voice . . .

"Why, Katy? Why get involved with him at all?" I asked, sitting up in bed to hug my knees. We had been friends a long time and I hated to see her marriage go bad.

She shook her head. "Bored, frustrated, I don't know. It didn't amount to more than a couple of drinks together and that was several weeks ago. I just did it because I was mad at Billy Joe."

"Dumb, Katy."

She laughed. "So what else is new? Anyway, you should talk. How come you aren't married to Sam? He wants to get married."

I shrugged. "We thought about it, but . . ." I made a wry face. "It just won't work. He is too, ah . . . I guess *protective* would be the word. He doesn't like it when I take any kind of a case he thinks is risky. Actually, he doesn't want me to do anything except genealogy."

"And you'd probably get into trouble with that," Katy said with a grin. "But how come you told Linda you don't run a detective agency?"

"Because I don't. At least, not the kind she meant. You know that."

"No I don't. What kind of a detective agency is it then? No, don't tell me. Let me go get some more coffee and a couple of sweet rolls. I'll be right back." She picked up the thermos and swished out the door. Katy never just walked, she had a sexy swing in every move.

By the time I'd brushed my teeth and washed my face she was back with a tray of orange juice, sliced papaya with lime, rolls, and another jug of coffee. We sat cross-legged on the bed and ate. It reminded me of our days in college.

"So?" she asked. "What's this about not running a detective agency? You've solved more than one murder, haven't you?"

"Well, yes, I guess so, but only because I was helping a friend. And the first one was because the man was killed in my office. Right in front of me. But you know that isn't really what I do. When George owned the place, yes, it was a detective agency, but we don't do that kind of thing. Not on purpose anyway."

Katy shrugged. "What do you mean, we?" she asked.

"Martha is we. You remember Martha. You've met her, I know. She's worked for me for ages. She's my office manager and a more or less partner."

"Mmm, yes. I remember her. Tall, black, drop-dead gorgeous, has an English accent, and orders you around like a deck hand. You never said anything about making her a partner."

"It isn't a formal thing. And I did tell you. You just

forgot. Anyway, after we both nearly got killed investigating the murders of Peter and Karl Johnson I've been a lot more careful about what kind of cases we take."

"Well, what do you do? You never say anything in your letters about what you're doing."

"It's not that interesting. We collect, process, and deliver information."

"What kind of information? What are you into, some kind of super spying?"

"Don't be silly. You know what I do. We collect any kind of information that is legally obtainable through libraries, genealogical societies, public records, anything like that. Information that is available to anyone who knows where to look and has the time and skill to do it. I've told you all this before, Katy."

"Still sounds like spies to me. Who hires you?"

"All kinds of people, but surprisingly enough, other investigative agencies call us a lot. Apparently it's easier to ask us to find out when and where someone was born than it is to find out for themselves. We do a lot of work for lawyers too."

"I seem to remember you telling me Martha was a whiz on the computer. Could break into data banks she wasn't supposed to, things like that."

"Good heavens, what ever gave you that idea? That's called hacking. Highly illegal."

"You told me."

"Mmm. Well, I should learn to keep my mouth shut," I said, making a face at her. "C'mon, let's go do something exciting."

"You're on. Drag out the swishiest outfit in your suit-case, heels and all, and we'll go have lunch at the cafeteria."

"Swish and heels? For a cafeteria? You're putting me on."

Katy laughed. "You'll be surprised."

Chapter Six

She was right. I was surprised. Not only by the cafeteria itself—an interior decorator's nightmare in ankle-deep carpet, crystal chandeliers, and a pianist—but also by the customers. Most of the men were wearing what appeared to be standard male garb for Del Rio: dark pants, white shirts, and wide belts with heavy turquoise buckles. The women, however, were dressed to the nines. I had never seen so many name-brand outfits in one room before, to say nothing of the diamonds. Every female in the place glittered like a Christmas tree. My violet and green India silk suit didn't half make the grade.

After we collected our lunch (a tamale with red beans and rice, fried okra and jalapeño cornbread—Katy said I had to try the local cuisine), we crossed the main dining area and entered a smaller room that was a little quieter.

"What's happening?" I asked as we seated ourselves. "Is there a big wedding going on somewhere?"

Katy grinned with delight. "Nope, this is just the regular lunch crowd. Isn't it a riot? It's so . . . so . . ."

"Gaudy? Tasteless? Silly?"

"All of the above, and then some. It's only a cafeteria, and the food isn't even all that good, but it's *the* place to eat, especially at noon."

"But . . ." I looked around. "The way the women are dressed . . . I mean, good grief, that gal over in the corner has on a diamond bracelet that's at least two inches wide! Or it looks like diamond, anyway. Do they usually dress like this?"

"Most of them, always."

"You're kidding me."

"Never."

"They weren't gussied up this much last night."

"I know. Isn't it crazy? This noon do, tribal ritual or whatever it is, seems to be a Del Rio special. I've never seen anything like it anywhere else in the Southwest."

"Aberration is more like it."

"I thought it would get you," Katy said, rolling her eyes. We both started giggling and were hard put to keep straight faces when a minute or so later one of the women I'd met the night before, Rosellen Ford, stopped by the table. Her lunch tray held a glass of iced tea and a mound of french fries that smelled heavenly. With her slender figure she didn't need to worry about fat grams. She too was dressed as if attending a palace soiree, in a wine-red taffeta suit with matching shoes sporting rhinestone buckles.

"You two seem to be having a good time," she said with an arch smile. She had beautiful teeth. "What's so funny?"

"Oh, Demary was just telling me about some of her cases," Katy said, her eyes sparkling. "She is a detective, you know."

I gave her a furious look, but before I could spout my usual disclaimer the woman turned to me and asked, "Well, you certainly came at just the right time then, didn't you?"

I didn't catch her meaning. "Right time for what?" I asked.

"For solving the murder, of course. You can do just like that writer woman on TV."

"What murder? Who?" Katy demanded.

"Why Gary McCall, of course. You heard last night."

The color drained out of Katy's face. "But it was an accident. A fight or something."

"Well, Orin Cato now says it's murder."

"How did you hear about it?" I asked.

"He told Keith this morning that it was a homicide and that the charge ought to be first degree. Said the weapon was a metal bar or rod of some kind and there wasn't anything like that anywhere around where they found him. He said . . . Oh, there's Donna. I've got to go. Y'all take care now." Rosellen trotted off, tray tilting precariously.

Somewhat surprised, I realized I'd understood her and everyone else this morning without too much difficulty. The accent wasn't as confusing as it had been, although I still wasn't sure what they meant sometimes. Such as her exit farewell. I asked Katy, "What did she mean by that?"

"By what?" Katy scowled at Rosellen's retreating back.

"The 'take care' bit. Does she know something about you and Gary?"

"Good heavens, no. There isn't anything to know. I told you that. That's just one of the ways they say goodbye around here. What I wonder is what in the world Orin Cato is talking about. What does he mean by murder?"

"It usually means the victim was killed deliberately," I said sourly. "Who is Keith?"

"Huh? Oh. Rosellen's husband. He's the assistant DA." Katy said absently. "But why does he say murder?"

He ought to know, I thought acidly. I had already decided against telling Katy about the fight, or the two men in the hall at the club. At least not now, it wasn't the time or the place. Another of her friends I'd met the night before, Betty, was heading for our table. Betty was a short, busty woman who reminded me of a pouter pigeon. She was dressed in a sleeveless linen dress with multiple gold bracelets clanking on both wrists.

"Katy. Demary. Have you talked to Wynona yet?" she asked, stopping beside us.

As I had no idea who, or what, Wynona was, I waited for Katy to answer. When she said she hadn't heard anything, Betty continued.

"Good. I get y'all first then. For barbecue Saturday night. All right? Unless you're too upset over Linda?"

Katy frowned at her. "Over Linda? Why should I be . . . I mean, what's wrong with her? She was all right last night."

"Katy! You haven't heard, then?"

"Heard what?" Katy demanded, beginning to lose patience. "What happened to Linda? Did she get in an accident or what?"

"She shot Gerald. Didn't kill him, of course, but still . . ."

Both of us gawked at her. I remembered meeting Linda Cameron and talking about the bridge tournament, but had only a faint recollection of meeting Gerald the night before. A pleasant, stocky man with a sun-browned face and sparkling eyes.

"What?" Katy gasped. "How? When? What happened? Don't stand there looking smug, Betty. Sit down and tell us what happened."

Betty sat. "It was right after Linda left the club. Gerald left a few minutes later than she did. They both had their own cars, and she was waiting for him. She followed him out to the Texas Bar. You know, that place out by the . . ."

"Yes, yes, I know where it is. Go on."

"Well, when he went in Linda took that old forty-five of her daddy's out of the glove compartment where she keeps it and waltzed right in after him. She knew darn well he was meeting that little blond from Carlsbad that he's been chasing around with. So Linda marched in and started shooting."

"Good grief, did she kill the girl?" Katy asked.

"Well, no. She didn't kill anybody. She shot the place up some, broke a bunch of bottles on the back bar and scared the bejabbers out of everyone there, but no, she didn't even hit anybody. You better believe she put the fear of the hereafter into Gerald, though."

I could certainly believe that. A .45 is one big gun.

"She should've winged him at least, nicked his ear or

something," Katy said after Betty had gone off to take the news to another table. "She could have if she'd wanted to. She's a good shot."

"Are you kidding? With a forty-five? She'd have blown his head off. What's the matter with you anyway, Katy? Gerald may be up to no good but that doesn't mean his wife should shoot him, for pity's sake. And how come nobody called the police? Betty said they didn't bother. What kind of a deal is that?"

"Nobody got hurt, so why should they? Gerald took the gun away from her and said he'd pay for the damage."

"Katy, it's illegal to go around shooting up bars, whether you mean to hit somebody or not. At least it is in Seattle."

"Oh, I suppose it is here too but Calvin knows where to find her if he wants her."

"Jeez!"

Katy laughed. "In some ways this is still the Wild West, Demary. I heard the other day that more drugs are run through this county than all the rest of the state put together, but as long as there aren't any bodies strewn around nobody gets excited about it. Now if somebody's cattle get stolen, that's a different story."

I wondered if drugs could be a factor in Gary's murder. It didn't sound to me as if they had much law at all around Del Rio and he might have been in a position to make easy buys. According to Katy, the southern part of Billy Joe's ranch was close to the border. Or was that his friend Leroy's ranch?

"What about Calvin Black?" I asked. "Isn't he the chief of police? Why doesn't he do something?"

"Calvin? He's not really the chief."

I frowned at her. "He's not? I thought that's what the sheriff called him."

"Oh, that's what he's supposed to be all right, but he never does anything. The only reason he got the job to start with is because his uncle is a big wheel in city politics and all the good ol' boys rallied around and got him into office. Billy Joe says he'll be out next election. Thank goodness. I can't stand him."

This didn't sound too good to me. I had been thinking of having Katy stop by his office when we finished lunch.

"Billy Joe has known him since he was a kid," Katy went on. "He says Calvin was in trouble constantly from the time he was ten or twelve. Got kicked out of school at least once a semester. His big brother was always bailing him out of some kind of a mess. His brother's gone now, died in a car wreck, but Billy Joe and Leroy kind of take his place."

Right then I decided I was not going to tell anyone, including Katy, about seeing the fight. I might cut my visit short too. Katy would be unhappy with me, but I wanted to be a long way from Del Rio before the so-called law had a chance to trace my car.

Chapter Seven

W e spent the next several hours shopping and drinking iced tea, stopping in different cafés with Katy's friends whom we met along the way. For only having lived here two years Katy had become acquainted with many of the local women. We were leaving a pricey little boutique when I heard my name shouted out.

"Demary! Demary Jones."

I looked around to see a long-time Seattle colleague, Carol Ann Guginsberg, in a state police car at the stoplight across the street.

"Carol Ann, what in the heck are you doing in Del Rio?" I called, astounded. The last time I'd seen her, little more than a month ago, she'd been a member of the Seattle police department.

The light changed.

"Call me at the office," she yelled, pointing to the State Police logo on the car door.

I waved my understanding as she sped on down the street.

"Who in the world was that?" Katy asked, surprised. "You never said you knew anyone in Del Rio."

"I didn't know I did. Last I saw Carol Ann she was working burglary out of the main office in downtown Seattle.

Another of Katy's friends hailed us just then. We stopped for introductions again and were invited into another little café for yet one more glass of iced tea and gossip. Although Gary's murder had become one of the main topics of conversation—word of the sheriff's conclusions having spread at the speed of light—I didn't learn much about Gary personally. Which wasn't too surprising. He was a "hand" and the ranch women, or at least the women in Katy's circle, rarely seemed to know more about the hands than their names. Their daughters may have had a different story, especially with a man as good-looking as Gary was reputed to have been.

Late in the afternoon, awash with tea, we returned home.

"The Hills are here," Katy said, sounding extremely surprised, as we pulled up in the drive beside three strange cars. "Or at least he is. I can't believe Nora would dare show her face around here again, no matter how tight Billy Joe and James are."

"Why not?"

"She tried to hire Carmella away from us! I thought Billy Joe would have a falling down fit when Bud came and told him. James apologized all over the place, said he couldn't believe Nora would do a thing like that, but Billy Joe practically threw them out of the house anyway."

"Who is Carmella? Sounds like a frozen desert."

"Carmella runs the house and is about the best cook in the county. She was off somewhere yesterday or I would have introduced you."

"Did she make those wonderful rolls we had this morning?"

Katy nodded. "Bud is one of her nephews. She has two or three of what she claims are either nieces or nephews around all the time. She was born here on the ranch, has never married, and as far as I know doesn't have any brothers or sisters, so where all the relatives come from I don't know. I doubt they are any kind of relatives at all. More likely illegals."

When we got out of the car we heard voices coming from the patio on the other side of the house.

"I'm going upstairs to change clothes first," Katy said, heading for the front door.

I followed her up, intent on doing the same thing. Silk doesn't wear well in ninety-degree weather. My suit was sticking to me from neck to knee and my feet felt like they were encased in a high-heeled version of the iron maiden.

I was out of the shower and pulling on a loose cotton dress with a scoop neck when Katy gave a quick knock and darted in. She held her finger to her lips with a soft shushing noise and leaned her ear against the door. In a moment I heard another door close down the hall.

"That was Billy Joe's Aunt Crystle," she whispered. "I

didn't know she was here. She must have shown up sometime this afternoon and has probably already bombarded
Billy Joe with complaints about how I let Carmella run the
house. Thank goodness Billy Joe doesn't pay any attention
when she starts that."

"What's she doing here?"

"Sssh." She signaled me to be quiet, her ear still to the
door. "If the old trout hears you she's quite capable of
listening at the keyhole. I hope she didn't see me when I
came scrambling back up here to warn you," Katy whispered.

"Warn me? About what?" I whispered back.

"About her! She's got a tongue like a bullwhip, and as
far as she's concerned anyone born north of Wichita is a
Yankee. I know your temper, Demary, but please, please,
don't take her on."

Katy's eyes were as big as soup plates.

"For pity's sake, Katy," I said, trying not to laugh. Katy
was used to having things her own way. "Are you scared
of her?"

"You bet your bippy I am. She terrifies me."

I patted her arm. "All right, take it easy. I'll do my best
not to rile her. You say she's Billy Joe's aunt?"

"Yes. His daddy's sister. She and his grandfather raised
him after his parents were killed. She spoiled him rotten as
a kid and still thinks he can do no wrong. And I think she
owns part of the ranch."

"You don't know?"

"No. But the way she orders Billy Joe around she must.
It makes me furious."

"Didn't you ever ask him? Or her? Does she live here?"

"Good grief, no! No to both questions. She lives in town in a huge big house she bought when Billy Joe told her he was getting married. Believe me, I stay out of her way. Come on, we better get downstairs." Katy grabbed my hand and pulled me out of the room.

On the patio Billy Joe was mixing margaritas and issuing fussy orders to a trim, middle-aged Mexican woman who was getting steaks ready to cook on an outdoor grill. Katy introduced her to me by her full name, Carmella Laveta Arsiaga. She had soft brown eyes, a gentle manner, and a warm smile.

A long table set for buffet service with bowls of potato salad, cabbage slaw, steaming pinto beans, and several kinds of salsa stood alongside the house.

I was introduced to the Hills—while Katy turned a no-ticeably cool shoulder to Nora. James Hill, a hard-looking man with light brown hair cut in an almost military buzz, told me they were neighbors. Or what passed for neighbors around Del Rio. Their ranch adjoined Billy Joe's five miles north of the house.

Del Rio's chief of police, Calvin Black, was there also. He gave me his big white-toothed smile and said how nice it was to see me again.

I knew it was dumb of me before I even opened my mouth, but I immediately asked him what progress had been made investigating Gary McCall's murder.

He looked surprised—Billy Joe looked annoyed—but he answered easily enough. "Don't know as I'd call it mur-der," he drawled, with a smile that was close to a smirk.

"More like an accident, manslaughter to my way of thinking. But I suppose, you being a private eye and all, murder is more to your way of thinking."

"I'm not a private eye," I snapped, trying to hang on to my temper. I was getting very tired of the private eye label. "And I'm not the one who said his death was murder. Sheriff Cato did. Besides, if it was a simple accident why hasn't the other man come forward?"

"Now, Demary, don't you go worrying your pretty little head about such things," Billy Joe said sharply, handing me a margarita, which I happen to dislike. "There's lots nicer things for you gals to talk about than someone getting killed. You're supposed to be having a good time here."

I swallowed a gulp of margarita, too flabbergasted to respond. I couldn't believe anyone, not even a dedicated chauvinist like Billy Joe seemed to be, would say anything so ludicrous. The man must consider me a total bird-brain. No one else seemed to think he'd said anything remarkable, however, and in a moment the conversation turned to cattle and oil.

Calvin finished his drink and left. Billy Joe escorted him around the house, returning a minute or so later accompanied by a slender woman of about sixty with a face like a slab of granite and the voice of an adenoidal parrot. Aunt Crystle. Her long, bony fingers glittered with diamonds.

Her first words to me were, "Oh yes, Katy's Yankee friend, the detective."

Her tone made it sound as if I had an unmentionable disease. If Katy hadn't warned me I would very probably have said something rude. As it was, I smiled sweetly and said, "Yankee? Oh, you must have me confused with some-one else. I work in Seattle but my people come from Nac-ogdoches."

Katy nearly gagged on her margarita.

I did have a cousin in Nacogdoches. He was a university professor. Unfortunately, he had been born and raised in Portland, Oregon, and was only in Nacogdoches for six months studying some kind of cattle disease.

Crystle didn't seem too pleased with the idea of Nacog-doches. She asked how long it was since I'd been home, which I answered truthfully. We just had different ideas of where home was. She switched to the weather and then to family connections. I answered the weather by quoting de-scriptions straight out of my cousin's letters and came up with some really inspired inventions when it came to an-cestors, parts of which were actually based on the truth.

Katy looked like she might faint but it appeared I'd won the match. Aunt Crystle gave me a chilly smile and swept off, looking quite elegant in her floor-length black dress.

"You're crazy," Katy hissed.

"Shush yo' mouth, honey chile," I hissed back between my teeth. "And smile. We're having a good time here, re-member? Anyway, I'll be long gone before the old biddy can check up on me."

"Don't bet on it," Katy muttered.

The evening progressed through several more drinks, which I managed to pour into the surrounding greenery, a delicious dinner, and finally an after-dinner cognac. An-other drink I dislike. No one asked me what I wanted.

It was getting on toward ten o'clock when Nora Hill

strolled over to stand beside me. She favored turquoise over diamonds. Her necklace, a gorgeous squash blossom, almost matched her eyes. I suspected her eye color owed more to contact lenses than to nature, but the combination of brilliant blue eyes and long, straight black hair was spectacular. She looked as if she might have some American Indian blood in her not-too-distant ancestry. After a few minutes of idle conversation she asked, "Did you know Gary well?"

"Gary? You mean . . . no, of course not," I said, startled. With one thing and another I had temporarily forgotten about poor Gary. "I never heard of him before last night. What made you think I knew him?"

"Oh, I just wondered why you were so concerned." She took a sip of her drink, eyeing me over the rim of the glass.

"I'm not," I protested. "Not concerned, I mean, I thought . . . I mean it's, ah, just interesting. Curious. Being as the man worked here and all." I let my voice trail off and turned away. About mid-sentence I had realized someone else in the group was listening, intently. I couldn't tell who it was but I could feel their attention like a hand in the middle of my back. I thought it might be Aunt Crystle but she was busy ordering Carmella around.

Nora said something else about Gary, but I didn't respond, and after a while she went on to something else.

"Isn't this the most beautiful place you ever saw?" she murmured, gazing up at the side of the house.

I had to take a sharp look at her to make sure she wasn't being sarcastic. I didn't see anything beautiful about it at all. In fact, I thought the house itself commonplace to the point of being almost ugly. I didn't say so, however. I had already drawn too much attention to myself and didn't need to garner any more by insulting my host.

"The ranch is certainly interesting," I said. "Raising cattle must be complex nowadays though. Do you and your husband raise cattle?"

"Some. A couple hundred head. James does hauling."

"Hauling?"

"Cattle hauling."

"Those huge big trucks you see on the highway holding two layers of cattle," Katy said, strolling over to stand beside us. "They haul them to and from the stock pens, to the railroad, places like that."

"Oh," I said blankly, trying to remember if I'd ever seen one.

Nora gave the house another envious inspection and wandered off to talk to someone else.

Katy gave me one of her mischievous grins. "Was she telling you what a beautiful house it is? She thought it was going to be hers."

"Huh?"

"She and James have only been married a little over a year. She spent five years trying to rope Billy Joe. Linda said she spit fire when she heard about me. Billy Joe never could stand her even before she tried to steal Carmella, said he'd just as soon take up with a sidewinder."

I saw Aunt Crystle giving me a speculative eye and decided I'd had enough Southwest hospitality for one day.

"I've done as much damage as I can for tonight," I murmured to Katy. "I'm going to bed. The heat gets to me. Make my excuses, if anyone misses me."

Katy grinned.

Chapter Eight

I woke up before dawn the next morning and lay in bed thinking about Gary McCall's death and the peculiar way Sheriff Cato was conducting the investigation. If he was one of the men I'd seen in the hall, and I was sure he was, why had he immediately told the DA's office it was first degree murder? Why not just let things slide, wait for the coroner's report, or whatever? The longer it took to start a real investigation the longer he and the other man had to cover their tracks.

The conversation I'd overheard in the country club hall bothered me too. Especially what one of the men had said: "The driver couldn't see anything from there." Granted, the accent was still confusing me then, but that was the gist of the sentence. So what hadn't the driver of the car—me—been able to see from where I'd been?

I played the scene at the gravel mound over and over in

my mind but couldn't remember anything significant, nor identify any of the participants.

I thought about calling Sheriff Tate in Valentine, Texas, telling him what I'd seen. I had a slight acquaintance with him because of the murder case I'd been mixed up in the year before. I also thought about calling Sam and asking his advice. Decided against both of them. I knew they'd think I was being silly, or hysterical. The murder case a year ago had also involved a dishonest sheriff. It was just too much of a coincidence.

And then I remembered Carol Ann. I could certainly call her. I couldn't imagine what she was doing in Del Rio, but if it had anything to do with law enforcement Carol Ann would know how the investigation into Gary's death was progressing. Plus she would know all there was to know about Sheriff Cato and Calvin Black. Carol Ann could ferret out more departmental information in five minutes than anyone else could do in a week. She had a knack for it.

Which brought me to the chief of police, Calvin Black. I couldn't believe he was quite as bad as Katy painted him, but why did he persist in calling Gary's death an accident? He must know better. He had access to the same information the sheriff had.

Was it the weapon that bothered him? In order to make a first degree charge stick the prosecution has to prove intent. Premeditation. A fight that gets out of hand, even a two against one fight, would normally bring a lesser charge, maybe manslaughter.

The use of a metal bar, as Rosellen had called it, didn't change the basic precept. Either it was premeditated or it wasn't. And if the weapon hadn't been found, how did the sheriff know it was a metal bar? Or was that just Rosellen's interpretation of what Cato had said? He surely couldn't have gotten a forensic report back so quickly. Besides, Gary could just as easily have fallen against something. Maybe the corner of that metal building I'd seen. When I saw them one of the men had been swinging a round club that looked like a baseball bat, not a metal bar.

And why was Billy Joe so anxious to keep me from talking about Gary? Because he'd hired him? Put him in harm's way somehow, and didn't want anyone to know?

Or was he worried about something entirely different? Something the investigation might uncover by accident. I thought about that for a few minutes and decided, yes, I liked that possibility. It was far more likely to be something personal. Maybe a woman he was involved with, maybe blackmail. There was no way of telling at this point. But he had certainly been in a hurry to shut me up and, when he returned from seeing Calvin off, he had Aunt Crystle in tow, all primed to attack.

There was no other word for the way she lit into me. The last two weeks had shown me that Yankee resentment was still alive and well in the rural Southwest but not to the extent she displayed. She had set out to make me uncomfortable.

About then I stopped myself in mid-thought. I needed to get a grip on myself and stop worrying about any of it. Katy's problems with Billy Joe, if any, were not my business. She wouldn't welcome my interference. And as far as the fight/murder was concerned, that wasn't my business either. Which wouldn't stop me from snooping if I had any way of doing so.

With all that in mind I was about to get out of bed when Katy tapped on the door. She came bouncing in with two mugs and a carafe in her hands and a big smile on her face.

"Billy Joe just told me he's taking Aunt Crystle to Midland right after breakfast to catch the Houston plane. She's one of the judges for the International Quilt Show. It's next week. So we're rid of her for a couple of weeks at least."

"She quilts? She can't be all bad then."

"Ha! She does make beautiful quilts. But she's still a miserable old witch." Katy gave me a slanting grin. "And you just about dumped me in the soup last night. If she'd tripped you up I'd have never heard the last of it."

"She never had a chance." I finished my coffee and headed for the bathroom. "So what's on the agenda for today?"

"We're going to play a round of golf with Linda and Velma Jean. And you better get in gear. It's already eight-thirty and I told her we'd be out to the club by eleven at the latest."

"Are you out of your pointy little mind?" I demanded, peeling off the oversized T-shirt I'd slept in. "I don't play a decent game of golf and you know it."

"Hey, come on. You aren't all that bad. It'll be fun. You turned Linda down on the bridge game. I had to say yes to the golf. She's springing for lunch too."

I scowled at my reflection in the mirror. I knew Katy. She loved practical jokes. She was up to something. I didn't have time to figure it out, though, so short of refusing to go I'd have to sabotage her fun as we went along. In the meantime, I needed to prepare the ground in case I did decide to leave early.

"I want to make a phone call," I yelled, turning on the shower.

"Go ahead."

"No, I mean long distance. I want to call Martha." As soon the words were out I realized I really did need to call, for several reasons.

"I told you, go ahead."

"Won't Billy Joe be using the phone? For business? I saw his office downstairs."

"He has a separate line. This is a separate one too. Both the main guest rooms have their own lines. We have overnight visitors all the time and most of them want to make calls to their ranch foreman or stockbroker or someone every morning."

That solved one problem. The next was a little more touchy. Even though I couldn't identify them, I really should tell someone in authority that there had been two men involved in Gary's death. The problem was, who to tell? Not Sheriff Cato, and not Calvin Black, as Katy said he was incompetent, but surely there was someone honest in one of their offices.

I stuck my head back out the bathroom door. "Do you know anyone in Calvin Black's office?" I asked.

Katy looked up from the magazine I'd left on the bed, an old copy of *Elle* I'd found in the bedside table. "Calvin's office? No, why? Why do you want . . . Demary, are you thinking of sticking your nose into Gary's murder? If you are, you better think again. This is still man's country. You go poking around asking questions and you'll get chewed up alive. I'm not kidding."

"Oh come on," I protested. "This isn't the 1800s, you know. I just thought . . ."

"Well, don't! Even if I knew anybody in his office, which I don't, I wouldn't introduce you. Honestly, Demary. People, and especially men, are different in this part of the country. The double standard is not only alive and well around here, it is the *only* standard. You know why that TV show "Dallas" was such a hit in Texas? Because the characters were typical Southwesterners."

She got up and flounced out of the room.

I took my shower and tried to think of another way to reach the right person, whomever he might be. If Carol Ann could put me on the right track, fine. If not, I was back to where I started: let the local law figure it out.

I dressed, made my phone call to Martha, and went downstairs.

There was no one in the dining room so I wandered on into the kitchen, where Carmella tried to talk me into eating eggs scrambled with bright red sausage, green chilies, and deep orange cheese. The color combination alone was enough to turn me off. We were still considering other choices when Katy entered the kitchen on the run.

"Demary, are you ready to go? I forgot to tell you I have to stop by the library on the way out to the club. I'm chairman of the 'Friends Of The Library' book sale this year and I have to talk to the regional chair this morning before she heads back up to Santa Fe."

Carmella gave a resigned shrug and handed me a wad of napkins and a sweet roll.

The library, a tan and red brick building with numerous windows, sat in a park-like area that took up over a block near the center of downtown Del Rio. The town fathers apparently believed in libraries as well as country clubs.

The doors had just opened when we arrived, so while Katy tended to her business I wandered around looking at the exhibits. Glass cases along the walls were filled with Indian artifacts, as well as handheld tools and clothing the early settlers had used. The walls held new and old pictures of Del Rio along with scale maps showing roads, oil wells, the airport, and many of the ranches. I found the Valentine ranch, dated 1874, right away. Seeing the distances and relative positions of some of the places I'd been to was interesting, as well as surprising. It was hard to judge distances in this flat country. With no points of reference, such as mountains or even tall buildings, you didn't have any feeling of how far you were from places you had been to or what the directions were.

Katy found me studying a map that covered the area between Del Rio, Carlsbad, and El Paso.

"We're going to be late," she said, hustling me out of the building. "Linda is going to be ticked at me. The club is always full on Wednesday."

Chapter Nine

Linda was indeed ticked. Her body language held a lot of anger, or maybe anxiety, but to my surprise she didn't have all that much to say. She and a beautiful blond woman, introduced as Velma Jean Scarber, were already seated when we got there. Both had alcoholic drinks in front of them, not the usual iced tea.

"I'm really sorry, Linda," Katy apologized as we slid into our chairs. "I got tied up with Doris Holmes, you know, the library chairwoman from Santa Fe, and I simply couldn't get away from her."

"It's okay. I changed our tee time to two-thirty. They had several openings. We'll only be able to play nine holes, but that's all right," Linda said, giving us a vague smile. "Would you like a drink first? Before we eat."

"Uh, what are you having?" I asked. I had only met Linda the one time so I didn't know much about her, but she certainly seemed more nervous than I remembered her being. It might have had something to do with her shooting spree at the Texas Bar, even though Katy said it hadn't amounted to anything. She kept glancing at the door every few minutes, even while talking to us. She almost acted as if she was expecting to be arrested.

"Vodka tonic. What would you like?" Velma Jean answered for both of them as she signaled to the barman. A tiny little thing, not over five feet, she couldn't have weighed ninety pounds. She had china-blue eyes and the longest lashes I'd ever seen.

"If you don't mind, I think I'll stick to iced tea for the moment," I replied. "I don't know what Katy told you, but I'm not much of a golfer. I haven't played in ages. Two or three years at least. I'll need my wits about me to hit the ball at all."

"No matter. We aren't tournament players. Linda arranged with the pro for a set of clubs for you. Katy? Your clubs are here in your locker, aren't they?"

Katy nodded. "I think I'll stick to tea too. What are we going to eat?"

It appeared that Linda had already arranged the menu. Fat rounds of beef tenderloin wrapped in bacon, stuffed mushroom caps, asparagus spears, and a gooey caramel dessert.

I wondered if these people had ever heard of cholesterol. And how in the world did the women all stay so slim?

In due course we headed for the first tee, riding in gaily striped golf carts with CAMERON RANCH painted on both sides. I wore borrowed shoes and a visored cap that kept sliding down onto my eyebrows.

The game started poorly and advanced into disaster. My first ball off the tee went an ignominious fifty feet, swerved to the right, and lodged in a bushy weed.

"You must have topped it, dear," Velma said cheerfully.

Katy giggled.

I thought venomous thoughts about childhood friends and went to retrieve my ball. Linda had presented me with three bright yellow ones imprinted with my name, so this one was easy to see, wedged a foot off the ground in the crotch of two small branches.

"Maybe you ought to try playing it," Katy called. "Instead of dropping it, I mean. You don't want to lose another stroke."

Setting my jaw, I jerked a five-iron out of my borrowed bag and smacked the ball with a baseball swing. It soared two hundred yards down the fairway and into the rough on the opposite side. Not good, but at least it was beyond the others. It was also in a depression that took me three strokes to get out of.

The first hole was a par five. I came in at eleven.

The game went downhill from there.

Twice we had to let another foursome play through because I was so slow; I lost all three of my beautiful balls, flung grit into Linda's face trying to get out of a sand trap, and nearly brained Katy with my backswing as I teed off on the seventh hole. The last was a dubious accident.

"That's it," I said, slamming my clubs back into the cart. "I'll wait for you in the bar."

"Don't be silly," Katy said, sounding a bit shaken. My club hadn't missed her by much. "It was my fault. I shouldn't have come up behind you. I didn't realize you were ready."

"It was nobody's fault," Velma Jean said. "Just one of those things that can happen. Come on, now. Let's—"

"No. I'll see you all later," I interrupted, and stalked off toward the clubhouse. I could see it beyond the next fairway. Rude of me, I knew, but by that time I didn't care. The thermometer had soared into the high nineties, I had sand in my shoes, sweat ran down my back, my clothes were sticking to me, and I was so furious at Katy I could hardly look at her. I don't know what she thought she was doing, but if it was some kind of joke it wasn't entertaining. Both Velma Jean and Linda had a five handicap. My dismal play had ruined the game for them, not to mention that I looked like a total idiot. She had deliberately set me up and I wasn't amused.

I bought a clean shirt from the pro shop, showered, had a tall, cold glass of lemonade, and was feeling more civil by the time the game was over.

Katy arrived ahead of the others and apologized straight away.

"I'm sorry, Demary. Really sorry," she said before I could open my mouth. "I knew you didn't play all that well but I . . . I didn't realize . . ." Her voice trailed off into an embarrassed mumble.

"Why? Why, for pity's sake? It really wasn't funny."

"I'll tell you later," she said quickly as Velma Jean and Linda approached the table.

Linda ordered a round of drinks and we sat chatting while the barman made them up. The golf game wasn't mentioned.

It seemed like a good time to bring up Gary's death again. At least it got my mind off golf.

"It probably had something to do with drugs," Velma Jean said without much interest. "Leroy said he saw him with some drug runners."

Katy frowned. "He did? I mean, how did he know they were drug runners? I wouldn't know a drug runner from a . . . a . . . plumber."

"I don't know."

"When did he tell you about seeing Gary?" I asked. "Before he was killed?"

The barman brought our drinks just then. Velma Jean didn't answer until after he was gone.

"The day before, I think," she said, eyeing me thoughtfully. "Why all the interest? I know you're a private detective, but why should you . . . ?"

"No, I'm not. Once and for all, I am not a PI." I tried not to sound as irritated as I felt. Katy had done me more than one disservice on this visit. "I have a degree in historical research. That is what I do for a living. Research."

"What kind of research?" Linda asked, coming back from whatever was bothering her long enough to pour a little oil on the waters. She seemed even more distracted now that we were back in the clubhouse.

I decided it was time for me to mind my manners. "I do a lot of work for insurance companies and lawyers. I collect, process, and deliver any information they ask for. I do some genealogy and I have a number of writer clients."

"What do you do for writers?" Velma Jean asked, also minding her manners.

"Last month one of my writers asked me to find documentation on the murder of Alfonso of Aragon, a crime committed in 1500 by Cesare Borgia, Lucretia's brother."

From the looks on their faces, neither Linda nor Velma Jean had ever heard of the Borgias.

"Right now I'm trying to document some cotton shipments that left Corpus Christi in the early months of the Civil War. A writer client is doing a family history."

"How interesting," Velma Jean murmured.

I shut up.

"Did Leroy say anything about those three dead Mexicans they found over by Guadalupe?" Linda asked. Reverting, I thought, back to the drug topic.

"Mmm. Yes," Velma Jean replied. "I think that's what he was talking about to start with. Although I don't remember whether they were carrying drugs or not."

"They weren't carrying anything at all, the way I heard the story," Katy said. "They were stark naked. Probably brought across the border over east of El Paso in a truck of some kind and died of heat exhaustion."

Linda and Velma Jean nodded.

I started to ask for more details but decided I didn't really want to know about any more dead bodies. There seemed to be a lot of them around for such a small town. I said as much.

"Who do you think you're kidding?" Katy responded with an unladylike snort. "I still get the Seattle Sunday *Times* delivered, and from the sound of it you must have dead bodies strewn on the streets like confetti. And anyway, those men over by Guadalupe didn't have anything to do with Del Rio."

"How about that woman last night?" Velma Jean asked idly. "She wasn't dead, of course, but still . . ."

"What woman?" Katy and I asked in unison.

"The one in the hospital."

"What woman?" we repeated.

"Rosellen didn't call you? No, I guess not. Some man brought a woman to the emergency room last night around midnight and left her there without telling anyone who she was or how she got hurt or anything else. The woman was in bad shape and by the time the doctors and nurses had her situation under control he'd gone."

"What was wrong with her?"

"Her arm had been cut off just below the elbow. They think by an airplane propeller. Last I heard she was still unconscious and might not live. Shock and loss of blood. Rosellen said Keith thinks she was on a drug run."

I frowned. "What makes him think that?"

"Because that's one of the ways they bring it in. In a small plane flying just under the radar screen. The plane lands out on the prairie somewhere, they transfer the drugs to a four-wheel drive, the plane takes off again and the truck heads for the highway. The woman must have got too close to the plane as it was idling or something."

I shuddered. The lemonade in my stomach was making serious attempts to return to sender.

Chapter Ten

I was still a little queasy when we left the club. The thought of getting your arm chopped off by an airplane propeller, out in the middle of nowhere, in the dark, was the stuff of nightmares.

I also got a nasty fright leaving the dining room. We came face to face with Sheriff Cato as we crossed the entrance hall. I froze in mid-step when I saw him, little frissons of fear racing up my spine. I don't know what I expected, he could hardly drag me off with Katy and the other two women right there, but fear is seldom logical. As it was, he merely touched his hat to us and went on down the hall to the exercise rooms. I managed to get my legs moving and we went out the big double doors to the front porch.

It was almost seven by that time. I had nearly forgotten the golf game but Katy apologized again.

"Demary, I'm sorry," she said the minute we were in the car. "I wanted to tease Linda. I thought you'd slow us up a little bit and Linda hates that. I didn't remember your game being that bad."

I made a rueful face. "It usually isn't that bad. I mean, I still can't play worth a darn but mostly I do better than I did this afternoon. It's this blasted heat. I'm not used to it. You know what Seattle is like."

"Yeah. And boy do I miss it. Right now I'd give anything for a nice soft rain."

"A what kind of rain?" I had to laugh at her wistful tone. "Rain is rain, and we get wet and darn sick of it sometimes."

"Well at least it doesn't come down in solid sheets like around here. Do you know a woman was actually drowned on the freeway in El Paso a couple of years ago."

"On the freeway? How?"

"The rain was coming down so hard it flooded one of the underpasses. Her car stalled and when she got out to go for help she was swept off her feet and drowned."

"Good grief."

We were silent for a minute and then I asked, "I thought Linda was one of your best friends. Why did you . . . ?"

She laughed, sounding for the moment like the old Katy I knew. "Oh, she is one of my very best friends. I just wanted to hassle her. Linda is so hyper she makes me crazy sometimes, she's always in such a hurry. And she's so funny about golf. Everything has to be just so. And she hates letting anyone play through. I knew you'd drive her up the wall. I should never have asked you to play golf on a day like this, though. I'm really sorry, Demary."

I waved at a billboard thermometer ahead of us. It read 101°. "Forget it. This heat is enough to fry anyone's brain, let alone a displaced Seattleite."

We talked about old times the rest of the way back to the house and were both chortling over one of our teenage adventures when we pulled into the driveway.

"What in the world is going on?" Katy asked, when she saw five cars stacked up. "Carmella wanted tonight off. I told Billy Joe I didn't want any company. I can't cook."

"Maybe they aren't dinner company."

"They are too. The Hills are here again. The hunter green Cad is Nora's, the BMW is James's, and the blue pickup on the end is Leroy's, Velma Jean's husband. She must be coming out too. Why didn't she say so? And, oh no . . ." Katy's voice rose to a wail. "That cream-colored Cad is Crystle's. She's supposed to be in Houston. Blast her anyway."

"For heaven's sake, Katy, lighten up. She's only an obnoxious relative. Everyone has at least one relative they can't stand."

"You don't understand, Demary. She isn't just a pain in the neck. She really is poison for me. She caters to Billy Joe's every whim. He's completely different when she's around. He expects me to jump when he snaps his fingers and speak only when spoken to. I mean, he's impossible. We're having enough problems right now, we don't need her around too."

I couldn't help laughing. "You make her sound like the mother-in-law in a stand-up comic's act. I tell you what, I'll see if I can keep her entertained."

"No, no, no," Katy wailed through a strangled laugh. "You stay away from her."

"I know," I said cheerfully, getting out of the car. "I'll ask who did her face lift. That ought to keep her mind off you and Billy Joe."

"I'll kill you," Katy yelled, chasing me into the house.

Looking back to make a face at her, I crashed straight into a strange man standing in the hall, nearly knocking both of us to the floor. For a second I thought he looked familiar, but then I realized it was only because he was about Billy Joe's size and dressed in the standard Del Rio male garb: dark pants, pristine white shirt and string tie with a turquoise slide.

He caught me in a one-armed bear hug. "Whoa there, honey-chile," he drawled, blowing his bourbon-scented breath in my face. "What are you up to in such an all-fired hurry? Pretty little filly like you needs to be more careful."

Katy, struggling to keep a straight face, managed to introduce us. "Demary, this is Leroy Scarber, Velma Jean's husband. Leroy, my oldest friend, Demary Jones."

"Oh, yes. She's the . . ."

"No, she's not," Katy interrupted. "She is not a private detective, and to tell you the truth she's getting a little touchy about the subject."

"Well now, that wasn't what I had in mind atall, Katy-girl. I was about to say she's sure enough the prettiest thing to come down the pike since you and Billy Joe tied the knot."

I thought he was laying it on a little thick. My looks don't scare the crows, but I haven't inspired any sonnets either.

We managed to extricate ourselves from his embrace—he had scooped Katy up in his free arm—and ran upstairs to change.

I took another shower, my third for the day. If I stuck around Del Rio much longer I was going to start growing scales. Pulling on the same lemon-colored cotton dress I'd worn the evening before, I trekked back downstairs full of good intentions. I would be polite, sweet, speak only when spoken to, and not tell any lies.

Aunt Crystle was the first person to greet me.

So much for good intentions.

Dressed in a black and white western pantsuit that fit her like wallpaper, she cornered me immediately and inquired what Katy and I had been doing all day.

I took a jealous look at her board-flat figure and wondered what activity would upset her most. Lying about my golf game was out, as Velma Jean would be arriving soon. I decided to concentrate on something safe.

"Nothing exciting," I told her. "We went to the library. They have a section on local history. Of course, there isn't much of it. There weren't many people in the county until the thirties."

Crystle stared at me blandly.

Nobody else was even listening. I tried again. "The maps were certainly interesting. I've never seen anything like them. They have everything on them, even the road leading to the gravel storage area where they found Gary McCall."

As usual, Gary McCall's name triggered a fast response.

Billy Joe arrived at my side with almost comic haste. I was beginning to seriously wonder why he didn't want me to talk about the man. This time he hustled me off to the kitchen to show me how Carmella made fajitas. Her evening out had obviously been canceled. She was fixing what he called a traditional Mexican peasant's dinner: fajitas, chile relleños with sour cream, roasted chicken with lime, three kinds of salsa, black beans, tamales in a cheese sauce, and guacamole salad.

I didn't say I doubted a rural Mexican ever saw a dinner like that in a lifetime and had probably never even heard of fajitas. At least not according to one of my writer clients who lives in the hills north of Guadalajara.

When we finally returned to the patio, Billy Joe pressed another margarita into my hand. This time I pressed it right back and asked for white wine. I was tired of being plied with booze I didn't want. Besides, some of the patio posies were looking a little frazzled from their dose of margaritas the night before.

He immediately sent the little Mexican girl who was setting the table for a bottle of cold Chablis. He was very nice about it. I really hadn't needed to be so surly.

Aunt Crystle appeared beside me again, but before I could think of anything creative to appall her with Velma Jean arrived and the conversation slid back to cattle and oil.

Chapter Eleven

I behaved with perfect decorum all through dinner and for at least a half hour afterward. And when I did get into a controversy I didn't start it. Crystle did.

Right in the middle of an idle conversation I was having with Velma Jean about Leroy's plane having been attacked by a "coughing spell"—Billy Joe's words—Crystle flat out asked me what political party I voted for.

Velma Jean swallowed a gasp, blinking her big blue eyes with surprise. I, however, rose to the occasion. I'd been waiting for my chance. The evening television news had been overflowing with charges and counter-charges of local vote buying.

"Well, I tell you what, Crystle," I said in my most dulcet tones. "I pretty much vote the Southern way, the way my old Daddy taught me. I find out which candidate will pay me the most and that's the one I vote for."

Dead silence greeted this sally. I hoped my dyed-in-the-wool conservative father never heard of my sacrilege.

No one seemed inclined to jump in so I went on, "I personally have never met an honest Democrat, or Republican, for that matter. That isn't to say one doesn't exist, of course, just that I've never had the good fortune to meet one."

"Them's pretty strong words there, kiddo," Leroy said with a grin. "Course I have to admit some of our local bunch do seem to be living beyond their means."

"My brother has never taken a bribe in his life," Velma Jean said in a high, angry voice. She gave me a venomous glare and stalked away before I could figure out what I'd said wrong. I had definitely put my foot in it again.

Crystle followed her, leaving Leroy and me standing alone.

"Her whole family is in politics," Leroy said, still looking amused. "Her brother is our mayor."

"Oh, no. I am sorry. Truly. I had no idea. How could I?"

"Forget it," Leroy advised. "Truth is, he probably is honest. He's too dumb to be a crook. And just out of sheer nosiness, is that really what your old Daddy taught you?"

I laughed. "My Daddy told me not to vote for any candidate who spent more time running down his opponent's qualifications than he did in stating his own."

"A wise plan."

It seemed a good time to bring up the drug running story Velma Jean had been talking about at lunch. I repeated what she'd told us and asked if he had any problems with drug runners crossing his property. "You are practically on the border, aren't you?" I asked.

"A hundred miles or so, but that hardly makes a difference. There could be a dozen mules trekking across the place and I wouldn't know about it unless they were dumb enough to be out there during the day. And even if they were, I wouldn't necessarily know unless I or one of my men happened to be in the same area and saw something we thought was suspicious. If they stayed away from the roads we'd probably never see them regardless. Actually, those three nude men didn't have anything to do with drugs. And they weren't Mexican either. They were three young idiots from NMSU in Las Cruces who bet some of their pals they could walk from Las Cruces to El Paso stark naked without being stopped."

"Good grief! How horrible."

"They must have gotten lost and wandered miles off course before collapsing. The state police had been looking for them for two days."

"As flat as the land is, I would think you'd be able to see for miles."

"It isn't all that flat. And unless you're up on a rise of some kind, you can't see much over a half mile anyway. And from a plane, a man, or men, are practically invisible if they stand still."

"Speaking of planes, were you hurt in the plane incident the other day?"

"Not even a bruise. Billy Joe's a good pilot. He put that bird down as soft as cotton candy."

That surprised me. I thought he'd been the pilot.

"I was looking at maps this morning in the library, wondering how you could just set down anywhere, but I saw there were dozens of oil roads that were marked for planes."

"The oil companies use small planes more than they do cars or trucks. Easier."

"I also saw a town down south of here named Valentine. Does it have any connection to Billy Joe's family?"

"Sure enough does. Billy Joe's great-grandpappy settled the place in the mid-1800s. Named the town after himself. It was some time later, in 1874 or so, when the family moved up here."

That took care of my calling the sheriff down there for any kind of help or information. He was probably a relative. The thought of calling Sam flickered through my mind again but I shook it off.

"I'm going home, Leroy. Are you ready?" Velma Jean came up beside us. She gave me a vague look, as if she was trying to remember who I was.

At the rate I was going, Katy wouldn't have a friend to her name by the time I left. I started to say I had just been trying to be clever, but before I could get the words out Linda Cameron came charging around the corner of the house.

"Billy Joe, you tell me where Gerald is, you hear me?" she demanded in a shrill voice. Her Liz Claiborne blouse was buttoned crooked and her normally smooth hair stood out in wisps all over her head.

"Huh?" Billy Joe said blankly.

"He was with you the last time I heard from him. Where

is he, blast him? I haven't seen nor heard from him since yesterday morning and he knew his Daddy was coming to dinner tonight. I didn't know what to tell him." The last sentence rose to a wail. She started to cry in big gulping sobs, her whole body shaking.

Both Katy and Nora ran over and put their arms around her. Velma Jean made soothing noises in the background.

"Can't say as I blame him for skipping," Crystle muttered.

Linda heard her, as Crystle had undoubtedly intended, and began to cry even harder.

Billy Joe backed away, making shooing motions with both hands. "Ah, what made you think he was with me?" he asked. "I haven't seen him since Monday night, at the club."

"You have too! He told me he was coming over here when he left the house. He said he had something important to talk to you about and then we were going to take a vacation. He told me to get tickets for New Orleans. We were going to leave tomorrow. And he knew his Daddy was coming to dinner tonight. He wouldn't—"

"Yes, yes, I remember now," Billy Joe interrupted. "We been talking about buying that Cross Ranch bull. But he never came, Linda. He probably stopped for coffee somewhere and changed his mind. He may, ah, he may still been, ah, some upset about you, ah, about your . . . ah . . ."

"No he wasn't," Linda wailed. "He wasn't mad at me at all. We made up Monday night. He knew I wasn't trying to hit him. Besides, he was on the car phone and driving down your road when he called me."

Both Katy and Nora started talking at once, trying to make themselves heard above Linda's renewed sobbing.

"I'm going to call the police," Linda said suddenly, her voice rising above the general hubbub.

Even I thought that was silly. Between her shooting up the Texas Bar on Monday night and what Katy had said about the macho males around here taking off whenever they felt like it, calling for police help seemed not only silly, it would make her look ridiculous. And would probably infuriate Gerald when he heard of it.

Leroy got into the act about then. He had been trying to stay in the background but now came over and led Linda to a chair.

"Somebody pour her a good big shot of bourbon," he said briskly. "Now you set down here and get hold of yourself, Linda. No sense in making yourself sick over nothing."

"Nothing! Nothing!" Linda cried. "What do you mean, nothing? Gerald has disappeared. How can you say that's nothing?"

"Linda, don't be silly," Nora broke in, pushing Leroy aside as she handed Linda what looked like a water glass full of straight bourbon. "He hasn't disappeared, and you know it. He's just gone off somewhere to teach you a lesson."

Shaking her head, Linda swallowed a gulp of the amber liquid. "No, I told you, we made up. He wouldn't do that."

I backed off into the shadows under a crepe myrtle tree at the corner of the house. This was turning into a regular soap opera. Everything was so larger than life: the people, their behavior, even Katy's complaint that Billy Joe was a woman chaser. I certainly hadn't seen any evidence of that. He was unfailingly attentive to Katy and I'd never noticed him paying any more than simple, courteous regard to any woman, even Velma Jean, who was alluring enough to draw any man's eye.

The scene going on now, with Linda crying, the three women crowding around her like a clutch of protective brood hens, Billy Joe looking more frightened than concerned, and Crystle and Leroy in the background scowling, couldn't have been bettered by a Oscar-winning director. Even Carmella got into the act. She had stopped in the doorway and was staring at Linda with a terrified expression on her face.

I decided it was a good time to visit the ladies' room.

Chapter Twelve

When I returned ten minutes later things had calmed down. Linda, more composed, was in the same chair finishing her glass of booze (as I found out later, a second glass the same size). Katy, Velma Jean, and Nora still hovered over her but Leroy had left. Crystle and Billy Joe were sitting on the far side of the patio talking in low voices.

James Hill wasn't on the patio either. In fact, I couldn't remember seeing him since Linda arrived. He had missed all the fireworks.

There wasn't any reason for me to stick around. I didn't know Linda well enough to help her and I had a feeling all the rest of them, with the possible exception of Katy, would just as soon see my backside.

Before I could say goodnight, however, Leroy returned and asked what I'd like for a nightcap. "How about some

Kahlua?" he suggested, steering me toward the tray of bottles on the end of the table.

"Yes, I'd like that. And then I think I'll head for bed. This heat wears me out."

"Been warmish today all right," he agreed. "Not late though."

I glanced at my watch. He was right. I felt like it should be midnight at least but it was only a few minutes after ten.

We sat down by the table. Leroy studied Linda with a jaundiced expression.

"You don't seem to be worried about Gerald," I said in a neutral voice.

He switched his attention back to me. "Worried? No, why should I be? He doesn't have any better sense than she does. He probably did go off to teach her a lesson. Silly cow, shooting up a bar like that. Linda is always getting all riled up over nothing. If it had been Velma Jean, I'd have belted her one. Gerald's too easy on her. Always has been."

I smiled to myself at the idea of him "belting" Velma Jean. In the first place, she was so tiny even a hard slap would knock her off her feet, and second, he wouldn't dare. Velma Jean had far too much spunk.

"Have you known them a long time?" I asked, keeping my thoughts to myself.

"Went to school with Gerald. Linda's from over Lubbock way."

"You and Billy Joe went to the same school too, didn't you? I think Katy mentioned it."

"Uh-huh. In fact, all four of us did. Me, Billy Joe, Gerald, and James Hill. Went to grade school and high school together, and as much college as we managed to get through."

"Were Calvin Black and Sheriff Cato part of the gang?"

An odd expression washed across his face. I couldn't tell if it was my questions or something else that caused it. At any rate, he answered pleasantly enough.

"No, Calvin is some younger than the rest of us. He was still in high school when we were in college. Orin is a couple of years older."

"I'll bet the bunch of you had a high old time."

Leroy laughed. "We sure enough did."

Velma Jean looked up with a frown. In a minute the four women got up. Katy and Nora took Linda into the house. Velma Jean came over to the table.

"Katy's going to put Linda to bed upstairs. I'm going home."

Leroy nodded. "I'll be along soon. I want to talk to Billy Joe for a minute."

I tried to apologize to Velma Jean again. "I'm sorry, Velma Jean. I certainly didn't mean to insult you or your family. I was just trying to be funny. I had no idea . . ."

"What? Oh, forget it. I have," she said.

I didn't think she had done anything of the kind but there wasn't much I could do about it.

I said goodnight to the patio at large and went upstairs. The hall was quiet. If Katy and Linda were in one of the bedrooms I didn't hear them, which was fine with me. I needed some time to get my thoughts in order before I called Martha. I had told her to expect my call around eleven her time, midnight here, still an hour away.

I changed into my T-shirt nightgown, got my notebook and pen out of my purse, and sat down at the small table by the window. The reflected glow from the patio on the north side of the house picked out the bulky shapes of the barns and sheds. A tall pecan tree beside the lane to the corrals cast fluttering shadows on the grass of the back yard.

Martha answered on the first ring. I was more than glad to hear her buttery smooth voice with its broad English accent. I was beginning to feel isolated here.

"Demary, what have you gotten yourself into?" she asked immediately, her tone sharp. "I've been on the computer for nine straight hours and the most positive thing I've learned isn't going to make you fall about laughing, believe me."

"What are you talking about? The only thing I asked you to do was check up on a couple of people and a couple of ranches."

"And Sheriff Cato. And the chief of police. And a dead cowhand. By the way, how's the weather down there?"

"Horrible! It was 101 at four o'clock today and I don't think it's gone down ten degrees."

"Enjoy it while you can. It rained here all day," she said in a irritable voice. Martha is from Barbados and the Seattle weather gets to her sometimes.

"Martha, what did Sam say, or find out about Sheriff Cato?"

"Sam's not here, so nothing."

"Where the heck is he?"

"Salmon fishing out of Homer, Alaska."

"What!? He can't be. Just looking at a rowboat makes him seasick. He doesn't even like fish."

"Can't help it. That's where he is. But I think I found out what you wanted to know about Cato anyway."

"How? You didn't try to access their computers, did you?"

"Don't be silly. I'm not that foolish. I got hold of Jake Allenby and talked him into calling Valentine. You remember Jake?"

"Yes, of course. He was in Sam's squad, and Sam'll scalp him if he finds out he's doing stuff like that for us."

"I don't think that would bother Jake, but he was a bit skittish about the captain ever finding out. At any rate, he did call Sheriff Tate in Valentine. I don't know what song and dance he fed him but he said Tate was perfectly willing to talk to him. He had nothing but good to say about Orin Cato. They have known each other for twenty-five years and according to him Cato is about as straight-arrow as they come. If Tate can be believed you have definitely got the wrong man pegged as the villain."

I scowled at the shadows outside. "I don't see how . . . It wasn't what I saw at the gravel place, Martha. I couldn't identify anyone from what I saw there. I saw him in the hall at the country club."

"You only saw his back. Or so you said."

"Yes, but . . . Well, anyway. How about Gary McCall?"

"Nothing. Absolutely nothing. He was either in a witness protection program or using a phony name. There is nothing in any kind of database anywhere that corresponds to the facts you gave me. No driver's license, no birth certificate, no property records, nothing. And that reminds me, one of those names you gave me, Gerald Cameron, he doesn't own Cameron Ranch. Linda Cameron does. Both her parents died some time ago and Linda inherited the place. She was apparently the only child."

"How about Scarber and Hill? And Billy Joe?"

"As far as I can find out, the first two places have been in their respective families since the early twenties and thirties. The Valentine ranch since eighteen-something. It was in Billy Joe's name alone but he added Katy's name to the deed shortly after they were married. No Crystle."

"Darn. Nothing seems to add up."

"Demary, you're plain silly to be getting mixed up in this. You've only been there two days, you don't know any of these people, and you don't have a scrap of backup. Make your excuses and scarper before somebody sees the Toyota and starts connecting the dots. You told the sheriff you came in on that highway, and at the right time. Unless they're all simple-minded down there someone is going to connect you and the car."

"No, they won't do that. See the Toyota, I mean. Katy had me stick it in an unused garage the day I got here, to keep it out of the sun. I'm not worried about it anymore anyway. What I am worried about is Katy. I don't know what it's all about, but something is going on that isn't right, and I hate to see Katy caught up in whatever it is."

"So? Do you think you can persuade her to leave? Talk her into it? You certainly can't force her to go with you."

"I'm going to try. Call me tomorrow morning, about eight, and let the thing ring until I answer. I'll think of something to tell Katy and get us out of here. Maybe not tomorrow morning but by Friday for sure."

Famous last words. Sometimes I can be so wrong it's awe-inspiring.

Chapter Thirteen

I sat by the window for a while, too wound up to go to bed, trying to think what I could say that would persuade Katy to leave. The moon had come up, bathing the yard and outbuildings in a silver-white light that turned the commonplace corral fence into a work of art. It looked so beautiful out and so cool, I decided to get a glass of iced tea from Carmella's refrigerator and sit on the patio until I got drowsy.

I didn't put on a robe since I didn't have one with me, and started downstairs barefoot in my T-shirt nightie. I figured everyone else was asleep. It was after one o'clock. The house was dark and dead quiet when I left my room so I nearly jumped out of my skin when the downstairs lights snapped on just as I reached the head of the stairs.

Since I wasn't garbed for mixed company, I shrank back against the wall and held my breath. Billy Joe, still fully dressed, walked into view and across the hall without looking up. I hadn't heard the doorbell, but when he opened the door James Hill came in. Frowning, Hill pushed the door shut, catching his jacket pocket on the doorknob. The jacket, a pale cream-colored suede, looked old and worn, as did he at the moment.

"What in the world's so important you want to see me at this time of night?" Billy Joe asked.

"This." James pulled a newspaper out of his pocket and shoved it under Billy Joe's nose. He pointed to a story on the front page.

Billy Joe glanced at the paper and looked up with a frown. "So? You knew about Gary. What's got your tail in a knot now?"

"The picture, Billy Joe. The picture. I didn't see the paper until an hour ago when I got back to the house and I never saw the man around here. Is that picture a good likeness?"

Billy Joe looked at it again. "Yeah. Pretty good, I guess. You could recognize him from it anyway. So what?"

"So that guy's name isn't McCall. It's Larry Morrison, and he's some kind of a government agent."

I couldn't see Billy Joe's face, but I could see the muscles in his back tighten. "That's ridiculous," he said sharply. "He's been working for me for a couple of years at least. What makes you think he's an FBI agent anyway?"

"Because I saw him in Dallas less than six months ago. I was staying at the hotel where they had the bomb scare. He was one of the people hustling us out of the building."

"You couldn't have. I told you he's been working for me since early last year. And what makes you think his name's Morrison? What did he do? Introduce himself on the way out the door?"

"No, but he did give some old gal in a fur coat his name. She refused to get on the elevator until he and his partner had produced some ID. I was right behind her. I saw him and his ID."

"I still think you're mistaken, but I'll talk to Cato about it in the morning. He can find out if he was or not. C'mon, calm down and let me pour you a drink. I think there's some Wild Turkey out on the patio." Billy Joe threw his arm around James's shoulders and led him down the hall.

I stayed frozen in place until I heard the door to the patio open and close, then raced back to my room. I didn't know what Billy Joe might be mixed up in, but I'd be willing to bet my bottom dollar he did know Gary McCall, or whatever his name was, was indeed a fed.

The muscles in his back had stood out in ropes under his white shirt, and although I couldn't swear to it, I was almost sure Katy had said Gary had only been working for Billy Joe a few months. What was going on? Was Billy Joe bringing in drugs? It didn't seem likely. According to Katy, Billy Joe had all kinds of money from cattle and oil. Why get mixed up in the drug trade? Plus, if Gary actually was an FBI agent he wouldn't be investigating drug running anyway. Drug enforcement was part of the DEA. Nor would he have been involved in a bomb scare. That was the sphere of the ATF under the Department of the Treasury.

Gary's death was getting more complicated by the minute.

I was still too wide awake to go to sleep. I knew there was an empty room along the hall that was right above the patio. If I opened the window I might be able to overhear what the two men talked about. Sneaky, and I doubted I'd learn anything exciting, but it was worth a shot and better than staring at the ceiling. Before I could put the idea into operation, however, I ~~saw~~ looked out my own window and saw James Hill walking across the yard and down the path to the stable and corrals. His talk with Billy Joe hadn't lasted long.

Katy had told me the three Appaloosas in one of the corrals were Hill's, but one o'clock in the morning was a strange time to be visiting his horses. So strange it didn't take me long to decide I wanted to know what he was up to.

I jerked on a pair of denim shorts, shoved my bare feet into my sneakers and was down the stairs before I could talk myself into minding my own business.

There were no lights on in the hall now, nor anywhere else, but the moon was so bright I had no trouble finding my way out the kitchen door and along the same path Hill had taken. He was out of sight by that time, which didn't surprise me. What did surprise me when I rounded the corner by the corral fence was the sight of one of Hill's huge cattle trucks parked in the barnyard. His name was emblazoned across the side in letters a foot high.

The truck and the men moving around it were fifty yards away, but I was almost sure one of the men was Leroy

Scarber. Hill was wearing the same light-colored jacket; I recognized it easily in the moonlight. Those two and a third man I didn't recognize were helping two other men up into the back of the truck. In a few minutes they closed the rear doors and stepped off to the side. Someone else started the motor and the truck began to move.

It seemed like an odd time to be shifting cattle, but what did I know? Maybe they were more docile at night, easier to load. At any rate, there wasn't anything illegal about it. At least I didn't think it was illegal to transport them at night, or to ride in the back of a cattle truck. From what I'd read in the Dick Francis novels it wasn't illegal to ride in the back of a horse van and cattle weren't much different.

Still, I didn't particularly want them to know I'd seen them or even that I was out wandering around at that time of night. I never claimed to be Fearless Fanny and something about the scene gave me the shivers. I backed into the shadow of one of the Chinese elms along the path, slid around to the back of the big trunk, and made tracks for the house.

Chapter Fourteen

Martha's call woke me at eight the next morning. My eyes snapped open at the first sound but I let it ring at least ten times. I wanted to be sure someone else heard it too.

I didn't expect her to say much, since the call was just to be my excuse for leaving, but she had a bit more than that on her mind.

"Demary, I think we have a problem," were her opening words.

"Oh, no. What?" I sat up and swung my legs off the bed.

"I forgot to tell you yesterday that Daniel Zimmer had called. You remember him?"

"Of course I remember him." I could hardly forget him. I had helped solve the mystery of his wife's death when her body had been found in his garage. The wife who had supposedly been killed some three years previously in a plane crash. Plus, he had recently been helping me find

88

documentation on cotton shipments in and out of Corpus Christi during the Civil War. He worked for the INS—the Immigration and Naturalization Service—but he had friends in the Customs Service in Texas who were kind enough to help me access old records.

"What did he want?"

"He called this morning and asked me to get hold of you and tell you to leave Del Rio as soon as possible. Immediately, if you could."

"What? How did he know I was in Del Rio?"

"You were going to leave this morning anyway, Demary, so don't get all bloody minded about it. And as to how he knew where you were, I told him yesterday when he called to tell you he had some additional information on Confederate shipping records. I told him you had already left Corpus Christi but were staying with a friend in Del Rio so I'd pass the information along in case you might want to go back down there."

"Never. Not unless I get paid a lot more than I'm getting now. This country is too darn hot and dry. My hair feels like it's been fried."

"Poor you. Anyway, this morning he called again and very politely told me he wanted you to leave Del Rio today."

I sat with my mouth hanging open, literally, until Martha asked if I was still there.

"Yes, I'm here. I just don't believe this. What in the world gave him the idea he could tell me what to do? I did hear last night that Gary McCall might have been some kind of a fed working undercover, but this is ridiculous.

You're the only one who knows I saw the fight. I haven't even told Katy, so how can I possibly be in any danger that Daniel Zimmer would know about?"

Martha made a rude noise. "Did you ever consider it might be the other way around? Maybe you're a danger to someone else."

"I'm no threat to anyone. I don't have the vaguest idea of what's going on around here."

"That's usually when you're at your most destructive. Maybe it isn't what you know but what you might do."

"Well, I'm not about to let Daniel Zimmer or anyone else tell me . . ." I stopped and thought. "No, you're right, I need to get out of here." I told her about the woman in the hospital with her arm chopped off, and what I'd seen the night before.

"I don't see any connections," she said thoughtfully. "You surely don't think Billy Joe is hauling cocaine around in a cattle truck, do you?"

"No, of course not. It was just spooky."

"Ask Katy about it."

I might have done that at breakfast if Linda hadn't been there. I had forgotten about her staying the night. The poor thing looked simply awful. She had on the same clothes she'd worn the night before, again buttoned crooked. Her eyes were swollen from crying, and although it did look as if she had combed her hair it was still a mess. She also had the mother and father of a hangover.

Katy was trying to get her to drink a cup of coffee when I sat down.

"I can't," she moaned. "It'll come right back up."

"Here. Better she drinks this," Carmella said, coming in with a tall glass of what looked like tomato juice. She put it in Linda's hand and closed her fingers around it. "Drink now. It will help."

Linda had to use both hands, but she got the glass to her mouth and took a swallow. Then another. And in a moment finished all of it.

"You be fine now," Carmella said. "I bring some breakfast. You eat."

Linda nodded weakly, but in a few minutes she did seem to be on the mend. At least she quit shaking.

Katy grinned at her. "Carmella's guaranteed hangover cure. It never fails."

"What was in it? It tasted peppery."

"A double shot of tequila, for one thing. Lord knows what else."

Breakfast, when it came a bit later, consisted of what Katy said was huevos rancheros, pina-anana and grits. Which turned out to be two fried eggs smothered in salsa, sliced pineapple, and a big dollop of what looked to me like cream of wheat cereal. The cream of wheat sat in the middle of the plate and was supposed to be eaten with salt and pepper.

I ate the pineapple and two of Carmella's wonderful breakfast rolls. Linda, to my extreme surprise, ate everything Carmella put in front of her. I made a mental note to ask Carmella what was in her cure besides the tequila.

Billy Joe came in about the time we finished to say he was driving into town and did Linda want a ride.

"No, my car is here, Billy Joe. I'll be all right." Linda didn't look at him.

"We're going to go get our hair done," Katy said. "And help Linda buy a new dress. For tonight's party."

Linda gave her a surprised look but didn't contradict her.

"What party?" she asked as soon as Billy Joe was gone.

"Leroy and Velma Jean's anniversary party. At the club. For heaven's sake, Linda, you can't have forgotten. Velma Jean's been planning it for weeks."

Linda shook her head. "No, of course not. I mean, yes, I did forget but only because . . . Katy, I don't care what Billy Joe says. Gerald wouldn't do this to me. Billy Joe must know where he is. He was about to turn into your road when he called me." She stopped, frowning as she ran her fingers through her hair. "No, I remember now. He was passing the state rest stop, the one about a half mile before your road, when he saw Calvin in his rearview mirror and said he was going to flag him down. That's the last time I heard from him." Tears started welling up in her eyes.

"Don't you dare start blubbering again, Linda Cameron." Katy reached over and patted her arm. "We're going to do just like I said. We're all going to get our hair done, we are all going to look beautiful, and you are going to buy a new dress."

Linda smiled weakly. "I've got a dress, Katy. It's fine."

"No! You are going to have a new one! As expensive and slinky as we can find in this blasted burg. It will do wonders for your morale. And we'll talk to Calvin too. So brace up, girl. Wherever Gerald has got himself off to, we'll ferret him out."

"Uh . . . one thing," I said.

Katy rolled her eyes. "Now what's your complaint? Do you want a new dress too?"

"No, but I don't think I'd better go."

"Why ever not? You were invited. Velma Jean asked you at lunch yesterday and she mentioned it again as she was leaving last night."

"Oh, c'mon, Katy. You're telling fibs. She was furious at me last night. I'm the last person she'll want at her party. I insulted her whole family."

"No, really, Demary. She did say to be sure you came tonight. As a matter of fact, that's what she's like. She can't hang on to a mad thought for fifteen minutes at a time."

Linda gave a shaky little chuckle. "Remember the time you and I and Sally Peters were having lunch and Velma Jean came along and sat down to chat? She rattled on as usual and was completely bewildered when Sally got up and flounced off."

Katy chuckled too. She turned to me. "She had totally forgotten the terrible row she'd had with Sally just the day before and couldn't believe Sally would still be mad at her. It was really funny."

I doubted she'd forget her being mad at me that easy, but what the hey, the party sounded like fun. And in the meantime I needed to set the stage for my leaving. And I also wanted to call Daniel Zimmer and find out what he was talking about.

Chapter Fifteen

I went back upstairs as soon as we had finished eating and looked up Daniel's office number in my notebook. Although I wondered why he thought he could order me around, I couldn't help smiling to myself as I dialed. Daniel reminded me of a puppy. It wasn't his size; he was six-foot-four, nor his looks. He had bright blue eyes and freckles, and a strong resemblance to a Norman Rockwell illustration. Daniel had the personality of a puppy. Always friendly, hopeful, and full of nervous energy.

He didn't sound one bit friendly when he learned who was calling.

"Ah, yes, Jones," he responded in a brisk tone when I identified myself. "I'm sorry, I don't have all the information in hand yet. I'll get back to you as soon as I do. Do I have your number?"

It took me a moment to catch on. Someone was with him. I read the number off, added that I would only be there another ten minutes, and that I could call him later.

"No, I don't believe that would be wise," he said, still very curt and business-like. "I'll let you know." He hung up before I could say any more.

Now what? I wondered. Did he mean for me to wait for his call? Or was he warning me not to call the office again? Whatever his meaning, if he was going to call back he had better be speedy about it. I couldn't wait for him.

I changed into a sleeveless buttoned-down shirt. If I was going to get my hair done I didn't want to ruin it first thing by pulling a T-shirt off over my head. Sitting down by the phone, I moved it to where I could grab it at the first ring. I didn't want Katy to know I was doing so much calling.

As it happened, I had just heard Katy and Linda go downstairs when he called back.

"Demary, listen and don't interrupt," he said sharply. "I'll have to hang up if someone comes in. I'm probably breaking a half-dozen laws, to say nothing of in-house rules. The thing is, you need to leave Del Rio as soon as you possibly can. There's a huge para-military operation going down in Del Rio within the next few days and it's likely to be dangerous. I don't know who's involved, but I do know the op has been shifted into high gear because an agent was killed. I got the information through the grapevine and can't find out much more without being obvious."

His tone was so severe I didn't know what to say. "I, uh, I appreciate the thought, Daniel, but I'm simply visiting a friend," I said finally. "I'm not likely to be affected by anything like that."

"You are on a ranch, aren't you? South of the town?"

"Well, yes, I think it's south. But what . . . ?"

"Demary, I don't have details but I do know that's where the action is supposed to be. South of the town of Del Rio and . . ."

I heard a door open, footsteps, and then the connection was gone.

I put the phone down and sat staring at the wall, trying to think why Daniel would be so concerned for me. We were good friends, but not all that close. My first thought, that the Valentine ranch was somehow involved, couldn't be right because Daniel didn't know where I was staying. He couldn't have gotten the information from the telephone company in the few minutes between my call and his.

Gary had to be the agent who'd been killed, but Daniel didn't know I'd seen the fight. Nor did he know that I'd ever heard of Gary. If Gary had been working for the same branch of the government Daniel did, the INS, he could know Gary had been working at the Valentines', but again, he didn't know I was staying there. And what kind of a tactic could the INS be mounting anyway? The INS was the Immigration and Naturalization Service. They didn't have anything to do with drug enforcement.

I was beginning to get a headache. It was time to ignore the whole mess and go get my hair done. It would be a challenge for whoever did it, as my curly locks defied any attempt to coerce them into a stylish "do."

* * *

Carleen, the chunky young woman who stood looking at me in the mirror as she ran her comb through my clean wet hair, didn't agree. She told me I was just "real lucky" to have such nice hair. She made a part first on one side of my head and then the other, tilting her own head back and forth as she considered the effect.

"I think maybe a high pixie," she decided. "We'll dry it on big fat curlers to straighten it out some first."

Satisfied, she drew a rolling bin of curlers to her side and went to work.

"You're the detective lady, aren't you?" she asked brightly. "We heard you was visiting Miz Katy. You going to the big party tonight at the club?"

"Uh, yes." I might as well quit denying I was a detective. No one believed me. I wasn't surprised she knew about the party, nor even who I was. Beauticians in a small town know everything that goes on.

"She's a nice lady, Miz Katy. You known her long?"

"My whole life. We started first grade together."

She smiled at Linda and Katy, who were across from us and already under hair dryers. "Those two are lucky. I think they have the only two husbands in the county that don't chase around."

I sent a roller sailing across the room with a jerk of my head. "Are you sure we're talking about the same people? I seem to remember hearing about an incident at the Texas Bar the other night that didn't make Linda's husband sound any too faithful."

Carleen laughed, her brown eyes sparkling. "Miz Linda,

she got that one wrong for sure. Gerald, he weren't having no affair with Debbie. She's kin. His cousin's girl on his mama's side. Debbie, she's having a tough time of it since getting shut of that worthless do-nothin' she married and Gerald, he's been helping her out. I guess he didn't want Miz Linda to know cause he don't have no money of his own and Debbie's not much account."

I swallowed my surprise and waited for her to go on. There is no place in the world like a small town beauty shop for information.

"His daddy, he farms a few acres of cotton, fifty or so, on the Texas side," she went on. "Gerald, he was rodeoing when him and Miz Linda met. Doing pretty good too. He come close to being New Mexico All-Around one year. Both him and Billy Joe was pretty wild in them days, but they settled down now."

"Wild? Were they in trouble a lot?"

"Not with the law. Not Billy Joe. Never. Way I heard it, Billy Joe's grandaddy, he was real strict about the law. When Billy Joe got a speeding ticket one time his grandaddy paid the fine all right, but he made Billy Joe work it out doing all the dirty jobs around the ranch. At twenty-five cents an hour."

I grinned. "Sounds like Grandaddy had the right stuff in him." She was almost through rolling my hair and I wanted to get her talking about Gary McCall so I changed the subject. "Sure too bad about that fellow who worked for Billy Joe. Gary something," I said in what I hoped was a casual tone.

"Gary McCall. That's a strange one all right. You'd think whoever was responsible woulda had sense enough to talk to Sheriff Cato by now."

"Did you know him? Gary?"

"No. He wasn't in town much. Too busy, I suppose, and hadn't had time to get acquainted yet."

So Billy Joe had lied. Gary hadn't been working for him two years. "I heard he might have had something to do with bringing drugs across the border," I said.

She laughed. "You can hear that about anybody around here. Certain sure if they're a stranger. And that means anybody who wasn't born and raised here all their life."

"Especially if they're a Yankee?"

She nodded. "Some of the older people still think that way. I never did hear anything about Gary and drugs though."

"I wonder about that poor woman in the hospital. The one with her arm cut off. Somebody said they thought she might have something to do with bringing in drugs." I was bent on getting some sort of information.

"Never know for positive sure but seems likely. She had cocaine dust in her hair and on her clothes. Most likely carrying a bag of the nasty stuff when she ran into the prop of the plane. She died last night right after they got her into ER. Shock and blood loss. Never woke up at all. Nelda, she's my cousin, she told me. She's a nurse." She stepped back, apparently lost in thought.

"Gerald, he might know. He came in the hospital right

after they brought her in. He'd cut his hand in that dust-up in the bar. There." She gave the final roller a pat and whipped off the towel around my shoulders. "Let's get you under the dryer while I comb out Miz Katy."

Chapter Sixteen

We had a good time buying Linda's new dress. Even Linda did. She hadn't forgotten about Gerald, but we managed to convince her that nothing bad could have happened or she would have heard. She was still not happy, but we eventually talked her into the shopping spirit and she willingly modeled a half dozen of what she called "after five" dresses for Katy's approval. I could tell she wasn't much interested in clothes, but to please Katy she was trying to have fun. And considering that she could spend any amount she wanted, her tastes were very moderate.

Not so, Katy. She talked Linda into buying a gown that was not only very expensive, but outrageously high style. It was a royal blue designer concoction that looked wonderful on her. She promised to wear it to the party and agreed to be at the club in plenty of time to, in Katy's words, "knock everybody's eyes out."

We parted, reassuring Linda again that Gerald would no doubt show up at the party tonight.

I wasn't all that certain myself. I'd done a lot of thinking under the hair dryer and I didn't like some of the conclusions I'd come up with. One of which concerned Gerald.

Pursuing that, I told Katy I'd like to drive through the rest stop near where Linda said she'd last heard from Gerald.

"Mmm. You're not sure Gerald has just gone off somewhere, are you?"

"No. Are you?"

Frowning, Katy shook her head. "I don't know. Like I told you before, Leroy or Billy Joe, or any of them, take off for days sometimes, but never without saying something. I always know where Billy Joe is going, or at least where he says he's going. Linda can get so worked up over nothing, though, you can't help but think his being gone is nothing either."

She wasn't very clear but I got the idea. I told her Carleen's version of the Texas Bar shootout. She didn't laugh like I thought she might. Instead, she asked why I hadn't said anything to Linda.

"What? What should I have said? I don't know Linda that well. To begin with, I don't know if it's true, plus she said they'd made up so I figured he'd already told her about Debbie and she just wasn't passing on that particular bit of information."

Katy muttered something about Linda being too thin-skinned. She slowed down as she pulled into the rest stop, a fairly large facility with two buildings and several roads winding through parking spaces separated by plantings of shade trees.

A lone car sat at the very back of the parking area, half hidden by a group of Palo Verde trees.

"Oh, no," Katy whispered when she spotted it. "There's his car."

"Whose?" I asked, although I was pretty sure I knew. Somehow I wasn't surprised it was there.

"Gerald's. The maroon Ford. Darn him anyway. Why in the world . . . ?"

"I don't know, but the first thing we'd better do is make sure he isn't inside."

A hot wind blew sand in our faces as we walked across the tarmac. Bits of leaves and grass stung my bare ankles.

The Ford was empty, locked, and looking perfectly normal except for dirt and dust. Shreds of debris fringed the windshield wipers and blew across the hood. It had been parked there for some time.

"We'll have to tell Linda," Katy said as we returned to her Mercedes. She stared at me over the top, her face puckered with concern. "What a bummer. She'll worry herself sick now."

"I'm not sure we ought to tell her. At least not right away."

"You think something has happened to him, don't you?"

"I think it's possible, and a whole lot more probable than anything else. I barely met the man, but from what I've heard he cares a lot about Linda. I think she's right. He wouldn't do this to her if he could help it. Incidently, what did you mean about her being thin-skinned?"

"Linda has all the money. Piles of it, in fact. The ranch belonged to her family. Gerald's family was and is dirt poor and she's defensive about the difference. She doesn't care about the money, but Gerald does."

I sighed, trying to think of some way around the present problem, but I couldn't see where we had much choice. We had to report locating the Ford. I couldn't just ignore it as I had the fight at the gravel yard. "I think we better find Calvin Black and tell him we found the car before we tell Linda or anyone else," I said.

We had tried to find Calvin earlier to ask him about seeing Gerald, but he hadn't been in his office and none of the other men there knew where he'd gone.

Katy got in and sat looking at the Ford with a taut expression. "No, not Calvin," she said finally. "We're out of the city limits, so it's Orin's jurisdiction anyway, and to tell the truth, I never did want to see Calvin. I don't like him, and I don't want to spend all afternoon explaining why we came out here. Knowing him, he'd be sure to think we had some dirty reason. He's smarmy."

"Smarmy? What in the world is smarmy?"

"Oh you know, one of those guys who is always perfectly polite, perfectly correct when you're around other people, but turns into a creep when you're alone. No, if we're going to tell anyone we'll tell Orin."

Katy was determined, and short of explaining why I didn't trust him, I couldn't change her mind. All I could do was hope he wasn't in his office.

Unfortunately, he was not only there, he had us shown in immediately.

"Ladies, to what do I owe this honor?" he asked, moving two chairs around for us facing him as he sat back down behind his desk.

I was intimidated before we arrived; despite his courtly manners, the sheriff scared me rigid. To use a silly cliché, the man was one tough cookie, and it showed. He reminded me of Sam. If Cato ever guessed I was the one who saw the fight, I wouldn't have a prayer.

I made up my mind, again, to leave Del Rio as soon as possible.

Nervous, I cleared my throat a couple of times, trying to marshal my thoughts before I spoke. Katy forestalled me. She was off and away before I could say a word. Talking so fast I wasn't sure the sheriff could even understand her, she started with the Texas Bar incident and proceeded to relate everything she knew about Gerald, his car, and why we went looking for it.

When she finished Cato turned to me. "What made you think Gerald's car would be in the rest stop?" he asked matter-of-factly.

"I didn't think it would really be there," I told him, honestly enough. "That was simply where he was when Linda last heard from him."

"He said he was in the rest area?" The sheriff looked from me to Katy. His face was totally without expression. I couldn't tell if he believed us or was merely humoring us.

His attitude angered me. I forgot he was probably mixed up in Gary's murder and answered more sharply than I intended. "No. He said he was coming to it, or had just passed it, and that Calvin Black was behind him."

Cato rocked back in his chair. "Did he say Calvin was following him?"

"No, he said he was going to flag Calvin down, or some such thing. I didn't talk to him, Linda did. You'll have to ask her what he said."

"Yes. I'll do that. Do you happen to know where Linda is?"

Katy and I looked at each other with some surprise. I think we had both expected him to put us off with polite platitudes.

"She said she was on her way home, she..." Katy stopped, then started again. "Sheriff, do you have to talk to her? I mean, do you think something bad has happened to Gerald? She's already upset. If you call and ask a lot of questions she'll think for sure that Gerald has been killed or something."

He thought for a moment, pulling at his lower lip.

"Have you talked to Calvin about this?" he asked.

"No," Katy answered curtly. Hot color suddenly stained her neck. "I don't like Calvin. I'm sorry if that offends you, but that's the way it is. I put up with him at the ranch because he's Billy Joe's friend, but that's the extent of what I'll do. I won't be in the same room with him if I can help it."

I blinked, startled. Calvin must have really done something crude. I wasn't surprised at her opinion, I just wondered why she was telling the sheriff.

Cato didn't seem surprised either. He nodded and went back to pulling on his lip.

Neither Katy nor I moved.

"And you, Miss Jones, what do you think I ought to do?" he asked suddenly, looking at me.

There was something in his eyes, humor maybe, that reminded me of Sam. I didn't bother answering. It was a rhetorical question anyway.

"All right," he said eventually. "I'm going to have to trust the two of you to keep quiet about what I'm going to tell you." He gave us a sharp look. "And I do mean quiet! Nor do I want you to repeat what you've told me to anyone else. Not even to Billy Joe. Do you understand me?" He frowned at Katy.

She nodded, looking confused. She wasn't half as confused as I was. His sudden, dramatic change of manner didn't fit what I knew about him or what we were talking about.

"Very well. I already knew about Gerald's car," he told us in a flat voice. "I spoke to Calvin about it. He was on his way to a meeting in Seminole when Gerald flagged him down, or tried to, and couldn't have stopped if he'd wanted to. At the time he thought Gerald was simply waving at him. Said he waved back but paid no further attention so didn't even see Gerald pull into the rest area."

He hesitated and then went on. "I am looking for Gerald, but I don't want anyone to know that."

"But poor Linda needs . . ." Katy tried to interrupt but he overrode her.

"Yes, and I'm sorry about Mrs. Cameron but it can't be helped. Not for the moment. All I can tell you is that Gerald's disappearance may be part of something else. Something we're presently investigating. Is that clear?"

We both nodded like good little girls in a macho man's world.

"Then I suggest you go about your business and get ready for your party tonight. And remember what I said. You are not to discuss any of this with anyone."

We nodded again. Katy was obviously bewildered. I was trying hard to hang on to my temper.

Chapter Seventeen

The heat made me gasp when we stepped outside. It was so hot the sky was almost white; the blue had been baked out of it.

"This climate is unbelievable," I grumbled as I got in the passenger side of the Mercedes. The leather scorched the back of my legs.

Katy reached behind her seat and handed me a heavy towel. "Here, sit on this. The air conditioner will cool us down in a minute."

Neither of us spoke again until we turned into the ranch, where Katy pulled off to the side and sat looking out her window at what was for once rather nice scenery. A rolling irrigation system sent glittering arcs of water across the alfalfa field on our left. Beside me, a herd of white-faced cattle looked at us over the barb wire fence. There was something soothing about their indifferent stares.

I don't know what had been keeping Katy quiet but I knew what my problem was. Sheriff Cato. I didn't see how I could be mistaken about him being the man I'd seen in the country club hallway. But now I wondered if what the men had been talking about had anything to do with Gary's murder. The accent had still been baffling me at that time and I hadn't really heard them too clearly either.

Between what Sheriff Tate in Valentine had told Jake Allenby and my own impressions after talking to Cato, I was beginning to have some serious doubts about my interpretation of the hall scene.

"What's going on, Demary?" Katy asked abruptly, still staring out the windshield. "Is Billy Joe mixed up in Gerald's disappearance?"

"Huh?" I had to rearrange my thoughts. "What makes you think he had anything to do with Gerald's disappearance?"

"I didn't until Orin threatened me."

"Threatened you?"

"Not in so many words maybe, but when he said I wasn't even to tell Billy Joe about Gerald's car he sounded threatening to me." Katy was working herself up into what my grandmother called a hissy-fit.

"Don't be silly," I protested. "I'll admit he sounded pretty positive about it, but he has some kind of an investigation going on and he doesn't want us messing it up. Maybe Gerald is doing some undercover work for him and he's afraid we'll blow his cover."

The last thought had just come to me and although I didn't believe it, the idea might keep Katy from talking if she bought it.

She didn't.

"That's dumb, Demary. I like Gerald but even Linda would admit he isn't the brightest guy to ever come down the pike. He's not stupid, not about raising cattle anyway, but he's slow. Orin Cato would never use him as an undercover anything."

"Well, whatever, I think we better do what he says. All he's asking is that we don't tell anyone about finding Gerald's car. Right?"

She agreed, reluctantly.

"What prompted you to say that about Calvin?" I asked. Cato's posture on Calvin had raised a big question in my mind.

She sighed. "I shouldn't have come on so strong, especially not to Orin, but I really can't stand the guy."

"What did he do?"

"Nothing drastic. In fact, I've sometimes wished he would. If he'd ever done or said anything I could put my finger on I could have clobbered him, or told Billy Joe. But he never does." She thought a minute, biting her lip. "He does things like help you into the car and manages to brush his arm against you as he closes the door. Nothing obvious, nothing you can call him on. In fact, the first time it happened I thought it was an accident. He says things too. Nothing raw, just suggestive. And in such a way you can't really smack him."

"You've never said anything to him?"

Katy grinned. "Oh yes. I said something. Finally. It happened one too many times. I told him if he ever did it again I'd use his guts for herring bait. And I made a believer out of him. He's stayed well clear of me ever since."

"But you never told Billy Joe?"

"No. I started to once, but in the end I decided not to bother. It wasn't as if I couldn't take care of Calvin myself," she said, making a sour face. "Telling Billy Joe wasn't worth the aggravation."

"How about Linda and Velma Jean? Does he pull the same stuff on them?"

"Probably. I know Velma Jean can't stand him. He won't be at the party tonight, he wasn't invited, but he will be at the club making himself obvious. That's the kind of stuff he pulls. All the time."

She stared out the window at the flashing circles of water. Multicolored rainbows danced in the hot air.

"It started years ago when Billy Joe and all the guys were nineteen or twenty. There were five of them then who ran around together. Billy Joe, James, Leroy, Gerald, and Calvin's older brother, Peter. One Saturday they all went to El Paso and took Calvin along because they were going to the bull fights in Juarez the next day and he had never seen them. I think he was fourteen."

She stopped for a moment, then continued. "They checked into a motel and after dinner left Calvin watching television while the guys went out on the town. They got back at one in the morning all pretty well lit, but according to Billy Joe, not really drunk. About fifteen minutes later Calvin came banging on his door in a screaming panic. Peter had fallen in the bathroom and cracked his head on the tub or something."

"He was dead?" I asked, feeling a flash of pity for the boys they had been.

"Very. He'd broken his neck. It was ruled an accident but somehow they all felt guilty, as if they could have prevented it somehow. And none of them have ever really got over the guilty feeling. They always lean over backwards for Calvin. They helped make him chief."

"Still? I mean he's a big boy now, and a lawman to boot."

Katy shrugged. "I think they all try to treat him like they think Peter would have done." She put the car into gear with a jerk, plainly not liking the subject.

"We've been doing so much running around today I forgot to tell you Martha called me this morning," I said. I wanted to get this over with.

"I heard your phone ring. What did she want?"

I was glad I'd covered myself. "She said my contact in Corpus Christi called and had a new lead for me. I think I'll go back down there tomorrow morning."

"What!" She twisted around to glare at me.

"Katy! Watch the road," I yelled. She was heading for the fence and a very substantial-looking post.

"What do you mean, you're leaving tomorrow?" Katy demanded, whipping the car back to the center of the road. There was an ugly sound as her right rear fender caught the barb wire. She didn't miss the post by much either. "You just got here. You said you'd stay for at least a week."

"I got here Monday and tomorrow will be Friday, that's five days. And anyway, you didn't let me finish. What I started to say was, why don't you come with me? When I've finished we'll swing on up to Houston. We can do some shopping, maybe visit your Aunt Pastene, whatever. It'll be fun." That wasn't what I really had in mind but it would do for starters.

Katy pulled up in front of the house and got out. She slammed her door shut and stood scowling at me over the top. "What's the matter with you, Demary? I'm not going to go off and leave Linda. Not until we find out what happened to Gerald. I can't believe you want me to be so heartless. What do you think I am?"

I hadn't been thinking at all, obviously. My primary idea was to get Katy and me out of Del Rio. I still didn't have any idea what was going on around here, but I had done some heavy pondering on the way home and had come to the conclusion that discretion was definitely the better part of valor. In other words, I wanted to make tracks for home.

"Maybe Linda would go with us," I said as we went inside.

Katy gave me an exasperated look. "Oh, for heaven's sake. She's not going anywhere either."

"Who's going where?" Billy Joe asked, stepping out of his office on the left side of the hall. "What are you two planning now?"

"A shopping trip," I said quickly, forestalling anything revealing Katy might say.

"Another shopping trip? Now why doesn't that surprise me," he said, laughing. "You've only got your arms loaded now."

I made a face at him and dropped my packages on the hall chair as Carmella came to the dining room door to say that lunch was ready.

Lunch was, as usual, delicious: icy cold gazpacho, sliced smoked salmon, and a wonderful fruit salad topped with a honey and lime dressing spiced with chopped cilantro. I could see why Nora had tried to entice Carmella away.

We had finished eating but were still at the table when I made the mistake of saying how beautiful the ranch looked in the moonlight.

"You weren't outside, were you?" Katy asked, sounding alarmed.

"Yes. Why ever not?"

"Snakes, scorpions, tarantulas, and all kinds of other goodies," Billy Joe said sharply. "You don't go wandering around outside at night in this country. Never."

"For heaven's sake. We were outside at night on the patio."

"That's different," Billy Joe snapped. "The boys use a powerful insect spray around the patio every day or so and snakes don't care much for short grass so we don't see them near the house, but it's still not a good idea to be outside in the dark."

"But it was so beautiful out," I protested. "I saw the most huge moths fluttering around. They were as big as birds. And I saw . . ."

"Beautiful or not," Billy Joe interrupted, sounding angry now. "You don't go outside at night. Understand?"

"I sure do," I said quietly, angry myself now. There are a lot of ways to tell someone to be careful, and snarling at them isn't one of the best.

I was about to tell him so when Aunt Crystle came in. She gave Katy and me a crisp nod, told Billy Joe she needed to speak to him, turned and walked back out.

Billy Joe got up and followed her without a word.

"You know," I said slowly, "I think that is about the rudest woman I've ever had the misfortune to meet. She was sure behind the door when they handed out southern charm."

Katy frowned. "I know I told you she was a terror, but she's actually very courteous as a rule. She has a thing about Yankees and of course hated it when I married Billy Joe, but the way she's been treating you is ridiculous. If I didn't know better I'd say she was scared of you."

I hooted. "Scared of me? C'mon, Katy, who are you trying to kid? She's been on my case from the moment we met. She's about as scared of me as a mountain lion."

"I know, that's what strange."

I finished my tea and got up. "Well, all I can say is I'm glad she isn't my mother-in-law, or aunt-in-law, or whatever. Right now I think I'll go up and lie down for a few minutes. All the goings-on have worn me out."

I didn't want to rest necessarily, but I did want to be alone for a while. I was anxious to call Carol Ann; I hadn't had a single moment to do so since I'd seen her on Tuesday. First, however, I needed to sort out what I knew, or didn't know.

Chapter Eighteen

On my way upstairs, thinking about Sheriff Tate, my mind jumped to Daniel Zimmer and thence by some weird mental gymnastics to something I'd heard on Monday morning before I'd arrived in Del Rio.

I'd stopped off in a little town a few miles south of the New Mexico border for a sandwich and something cold to drink. The waitress had been less than friendly and after taking my order asked, "You one of them social workers here to take care of them Mexican babies?"

I turned and looked behind myself before I answered. I thought she must be talking to someone else.

"No, I'm not. I'm just driving through," I had assured her.

She gave me a further critical examination before going to get my glass of iced tea. When she came back again with my BLT I asked her what made her think I was a social worker.

"Your car got Washington plates."

This didn't make much sense but I nodded anyway.

She went on, "The FBI guys thought they had talked them white-supremists, or whatever they call them, into letting the women and kids out but all they let go was two young-uns and four little bitty ones. The babies are being took care of over to the hospital but I heard there was some woman coming from Washington to take them away. They's all illegals of course."

"Uh, I guess I don't know what you're talking about," I said, trying to sound apologetic and interested at the same time. "I'm from Washington state, not Washington, DC. I didn't know there were any white supremists around here."

"Huh? Didn't you never hear of the Branch Davidians in Waco?"

"Yes, but I guess I didn't realize . . ."

"Same kind of a bunch bought the old Penniwait place out by the river a couple years ago. Been farming it. They never bothered nobody and we never bothered them. Then, couple of weeks ago, the FBI comes tromping in talking about them bringing in Mexicans. Claim they was keepin' the Mex as slaves. Been nothing but trouble ever since."

A couple of truckers had come in about that time so I'd not talked to the waitress again, and hadn't thought of our conversation again until now.

Was that what this was all about? Illegals?

I thought about the cattle truck I'd seen in the yard the night before.

The men I'd seen getting into the back of the truck could have been Mexicans. That was not only possible, it was darn near a certainty. Which meant Billy Joe was part of what was going on.

Aunt Crystle's behavior made sense now too. She wanted to make me uncomfortable enough to leave. She didn't know me. Her performance was guaranteed to make me stay, not leave. Billy Joe was her pride and joy, and although she might not know anything about Gary's death, she certainly knew everything that went on around the ranch. If Billy Joe was bringing in illegals she would know it. Undoubtedly did. Katy had told me that Crystle always employed several Mexican girls around her house. And that she usually sent them to school. To learn English? Carmella and her numerous "relatives" were probably in on it too.

Maybe their motives were pure as bottled water but bringing in illegals was just that. Illegal. And from what I'd read in the Austin paper, smuggling Mexicans across the border could be a very ugly business. The people were crammed into impossible places: automobile trunks, barrels, underneath the floorboards of vans and trucks, even in shipping crates. Many died en route.

I sat looking out the window for a few minutes trying to reorganize what I knew, or guessed, from this different viewpoint. Illegals, not drugs. The only way I can do that kind of thing, however, is on my computer. My mind wants to jump around with facts. Seeing the words on screen seems to keep the facts in the right order.

I got my laptop out and started with the fight, typing in what I'd seen first. Three men, none of whom I had seen clearly enough to identify, had been fighting. One man had been wielding a club or stick of some kind. That man could have been Gary. I had no way of knowing.

I sat with my hands poised over the keys, but try as I might I couldn't remember anything else about the men. Nothing. Not size, height, clothes, nothing.

Okay. So much for the fight. What next?

Next had to be Billy Joe and his scraped hand. If he had been flying the plane, as Leroy said, how had his knuckles gotten scraped? His sore shoulder was consistent with a rough landing, but, in Leroy's words, the landing had been as soft as cotton candy. Leroy hadn't even gotten a bruise. So how had Billy Joe come by his injuries?

Billy Joe's shirt came next. His pants were dusty when he arrived at the club that night but his shirt was brand spanking clean. How had that happened? He said he hadn't been home.

The side of the metal building I'd seen beyond the sand mound, or thought I'd seen, might not have been a building at all. It could easily have been part of a plane. If Billy Joe had flown below the radar screen, as the woman whose arm had been cut off had probably done, they could have left the runway and flown directly to the gravel storage without much chance of being detected. According to the map in the library, the gravel place and the airport were in a direct line and less than ten miles apart, with few buildings of any kind in between. It was possible. Not provable at this point, maybe not even probable, but certainly possible.

I needed to get back there somehow and check out the place.

On the proven side, anything to do with Gary McCall made Billy Joe nervous. Very nervous. Then there was the Gary McCall/Larry Morrison question. Was he the agent Daniel had referred to, a federal agent of some kind? Yes. It would be too much of a coincidence to have two agents killed in the area at the same time. And if he was, what was he investigating?

The big question though was, why had Gary been killed? What had he found out? Something about drugs or illegals were the most obvious answers, but which, and what, specifically?

And what had happened to Gerald? Finding his car put his disappearance in an entirely different category. He hadn't gone off anywhere to teach Linda a lesson; something had happened to him. Or, as I had suggested but not really meant at the time, he could be on some kind of covert mission.

Last, but certainly not least, the puzzle of Sheriff Cato. I had been so sure, so very sure, that he was the man I'd seen in the hall. I wasn't now. Why had he cautioned us so strongly about talking to anyone, including Linda and Billy Joe? I had to suppose the sheriff was involved in the action Daniel had warned me about, but still . . .

Something about Daniel had been nagging at my mind all afternoon. It suddenly kicked into place. Daniel was with the INS.

Gary hadn't been investigating drug running. He'd been investigating the smuggling of Mexican nationals into the United States. Which could certainly have to do with the standoff at the Penniwait ranch. Was that what this was all about?

Scowling, I shut the laptop off and put it away. I was beginning to think in circles.

I picked up the phone and dialed the local state police number. To my surprise, the switchboard operator put me through to Carol Ann without even asking my name.

"I told her I was expecting a call from someone who sounds like I do," Carol Ann told me when I asked about it. "She says I have an accent. Can you believe that?" She giggled.

I had to smile at that myself. But from the switchboard operator's point of view I suppose we did have accents.

"What in the world are you doing down here?" I asked. "You surely haven't quit, have you? I thought you just got a promotion."

"I did. That's why I'm down here. I've been trying to get into the crisis squad for ages and I finally made it. I took two years of hostage psychology in college."

"Well, great, but what's that got to do with you being down here?"

"Oh. I thought you knew. The New Mexico state police have a special program on hostage negotiation. They run a class twice a year and take three out-of-state officers every session. The captain told me to apply and I got lucky."

"How's it working out?"

"Great. It's a super program."

"Do you see much of the city or county men?"

"Very little. There's a big flap on right now to do with bringing in illegals. The feds have . . . hold on."

The line went dead, and stayed dead for nearly a minute before Carol Ann came back.

"Demary, I've got to hang up. Can I meet you somewhere for coffee in about forty-five minutes?"

"The cafeteria?" I knew how to get there.

"Great. See you there." She hung the phone up with a crash.

I thought about borrowing Katy's car but decided not to. I'd use my own. The chance of anyone spotting me was almost nil and I'd be on my way out of here tomorrow morning, hopefully with Katy beside me.

Katy was my biggest problem. Should I tell her what I knew, and or guessed?

No. I couldn't. Despite her complaints about Billy Joe, she loved him. I simply couldn't accuse him of being mixed up in a smuggling ring, or a murder, without proof. And I couldn't leave her to face the situation here by herself.

On the other hand, if I didn't warn her and she was caught in whatever went down I'd never forgive myself. To say nothing of not wanting to get involved in an INS police action myself. Especially not, as Daniel had said it might be dangerous.

I was, as the saying went, between a rock and a hard place.

Chapter Nineteen

There was no one around when I went downstairs, not even Carmella in the kitchen, which relieved me of having to think up an excuse for going out again.

I wrote a quick note and left it on the hall table, weighing it down with a black and white Zuni pottery jar full of dried flowers.

The small shed where I'd left the Toyota was shaded by a huge old elm tree but it was still as hot as an oven inside. Too warm for the Toyota's old motor. The carburetor wasn't adjusted for the temperature or the altitude. Del Rio was 3,000 feet above sea level. It took me several tries to get it started and I thought for sure Katy would hear and come out to ask where I was going, and why. I didn't want to explain. However, neither she nor anyone else came running and eventually I was on my way.

I found the cafeteria without any trouble, parked in the

most secluded spot I could find, between two big vans, and went inside. Carol Ann wasn't there yet so I got two glasses of iced tea and settled at a table in the corner.

Carol Ann and I are close friends, but we don't socialize much, mostly because of the hours we work. We enjoy each other's company when we do get together, though. She's an outdoors kind of person, nearly six feet tall, with green eyes, short dark hair, and a casual attitude toward departmental information.

She came in and greeted me now with a big smile.

"Hi, Demary. Isn't this fun? I sure never expected to see you down here."

We chatted back and forth for a few minutes, catching up on how we came to be in Del Rio, before I happened to mention Katy's name and where I was staying.

"The Valentine place? Isn't that where the INS man was working?" Carol Ann asked. "The one they found dead out at the gravel dump?"

I nodded, pleased to have one of my speculations confirmed. Carol Ann took it for granted that I knew more than I did. "If you mean Gary McCall, yes. Or I guess his real name was Larry Morrison. What do you know about the murder? Anything?"

"Not really." Carol Ann took a swallow of tea. "There hasn't been much talk around the office and we're all too busy to listen to local stuff anyway. I did hear he was working undercover on the same situation we're studying across the border in Texas."

"The standoff around the Penniwait place?"

She nodded.

"What do you mean, studying?"

"We aren't taking part in it, the class I mean, but the captain gets an update every morning and uses it for demo purposes. The feds and the Texas authorities are handling it, although the New Mexico state police and some of this county's men are in on the action because the ranch crosses the state line. The Penniwait ranch house is only about eight miles from here. It's just over the line. How do you know about it, anyway? The whole operation is supposed to be classified."

"I don't know much. Just a few bits and pieces I've put together for myself. Have you heard if they have a suspect in Gary's murder yet?"

"Not that I've heard about. They do know there were at least two men involved, besides Gary, and they found the murder weapon. The perp used a short length of drill pipe." She laughed, shaking her head. "He wiped it off and tossed it back where they think he picked it up to start with. There's a big pile of old oil field stuff over by the fence."

"What's so funny about that?"

Carol Ann laughed again. I'd forgotten her primitive sense of humor.

"Well, if he hadn't tried to clean it they probably never would have spotted it. As it was, the dumb guy rinsed it off with a can of beer and tossed the can into the pile along with the pipe. One of the men saw the can and started looking around. Didn't even need forensics to detect the blood. A sharp old boy named Cato is heading the investigation and from what I've heard he's like the Mounties. Always gets his man."

I wondered if the killers were all that dumb, or if at least one of them knew he'd never be suspected.

"Speaking of men, do you know anything about the chief of police, Calvin Black?" I asked.

"Not really. What gossip I've heard has made him out a first class jerk, but it's all personal. I understand one of the women in his office is even talking about a sexual harassment suit, but again, personal, nothing about his competence. Political pull seems to have put him in office and you know how that goes. He'll be there from now on unless he does something really raw." She checked her watch and stood up. "I saw him just now as I came in."

"What was he doing?" I asked quickly, feeling my nerves give an anxious twitch. Although why I should be nervous of him, I didn't know.

"Just cruising the parking lot. I've got to go, Demary. How much longer are you going to be in town?"

"I'm going to try to leave tomorrow morning. One other thing I wanted to ask you. Have you been out to the crime scene? Are there any buildings near those sand and gravel mounds?"

Carol Ann eyed me sharply. "Why do you want to know that?"

I started to answer but she held up her hand to stop me.

"No, don't tell me, I don't want to know. The murder is a local problem and I don't want to know anything about it. But to answer your question, yes, there's a big metal building at the back, right on the edge of the arroyo that runs along behind the place."

She got up and stood a moment, settling her bag across

her shoulder. "If you're sticking your nose in McCall's murder, Demary, be careful. There are a lot of rough types on the scene."

She gave me a quick smile and marched out. I watched her cross the room and pass through the door. I seemed to be getting warned off every time I turned around.

Katy met me in the front hall when I got back to the house. She looked as if she had been crying.

"Demary, where have you been? Come talk to Billy Joe. He says someone shot at us. He's furious at me and wants to know where we went and what we were doing all morning." Her voice dropped to a gasping whisper. "I've got to tell him about . . ."

"No, you don't! You shut up. I'll talk to him. But what in the world makes him think somebody shot . . ."

She grabbed my arm and pulled me down the hall. "Just come. He's out back. You tell him we didn't go anywhere except to town. Nobody shot at us."

Billy Joe was in the side yard talking to a lanky young Mexican in muddy jeans and rubber boots. As soon as he saw us he waved the young man off toward the stables and came striding across the grass to us, looking very upset.

Fortunately, I interpreted his expression as concern rather than outrage. I had been all prepared to give him a piece of my mind, dictatorial males not being my favorite species, but he was obviously worried, or frightened, or both. Not angry.

I also had a flash of memory. "Is there a graze, or hole, or something on the back of the car somewhere?" I asked before Billy Joe could speak.

He gave me a hard scrutiny before answering. "Yes. And how do you . . . ?"

"I think I know when it happened," I interrupted. I turned to Katy. "You remember when we were on the way home when you, ah, looked over at me and the car swerved? The metallic sound we heard as you straightened out? Just down the road from where you turn into your drive? When we came back from town?"

She frowned, puzzled. "Yes, of course I do, but . . . I thought I clipped the fence with the fender.

"Is it a barb wire scratch?" she asked Billy Joe. She started running back around the house without waiting for an answer. I followed.

The Mercedes had a bright shiny groove, not on the fender where I expected it, but on the metal upright between the side and rear windows. Head high for anyone seated in the car.

It was no barb wire scratch, that was for sure.

Chapter Twenty

To my surprise, after we looked at the car and again described what happened and where, Billy Joe's demeanor went through a remarkably quick change. As did Katy's. She gave a sigh of relief, losing her beleaguered air immediately. Billy Joe was still upset but no longer worried or frightened. Instead, he was mad.

It seemed the neighbor had a boy who was entirely too careless with his rifle and Billy Joe went stomping into his office to give the man a call.

The atmosphere changed so rapidly it took me several minutes to catch up.

"Has the boy shot something or somebody before?" I asked, still not understanding why the gunshot was now all right.

"What? Oh, yes. He's had a couple of accidents," Katy said, sounding much more cheerful.

"Accidents? What kind of accidents? Katy, what's the deal here? Why was Billy Joe angry and now he's not? Or at least not at us."

Katy gave me a blank look, biting her lip. "I don't know," she said finally. "The thing is, if it was just Ralph being careless again, no one was shooting at us. You and me. It was nothing we did. Billy Joe thought . . . I don't know why he . . ." She stopped and started again. "Ralph creased one of our steers last year and his daddy said he would take his rifle away from him, but maybe he gave it back to him by now."

"I still don't understand. Why is it all right for Ralph to take a shot at us but it's not all right for anyone else?" I asked.

"It's not 'all right' for him to shoot at us. Don't be silly. Ralph wouldn't have done it deliberately. He was probably potting jack rabbits or something."

"With a rifle? Where there are people and cattle around?" My voice rose to a squeak. "How old is this kid, anyway?"

"Ralph? Nine or ten, I think."

I was too dumbfounded to answer. Between women who shot up bars and nine-year-old kids with rifles Del Rio struck me as a plain dangerous place to live.

Katy said, "Oh pooh. Seattle and King County have more shootings every day than this whole state gets in a year."

Ignoring my protest, she changed the subject, chattering on about the party and asking what I was going to wear.

Again, it took me several minutes to catch up. Katy was still very nervous but she didn't want me to know it, so there was no use in asking her what the problem was or why she was worried.

This shooting business was the last straw as far as I was concerned. Maybe the kid had done it, but I wasn't going to bet my life on that possibility. Sometime between now and tomorrow morning I'd have to get Katy aside and try again to persuade her to come to Houston with me. I'd have to tell her why, and I knew she wouldn't like what I'd have to say, but Katy wasn't a fool. If I could convince her Billy Joe was mixed up in something illegal, or dangerous, or both, she might be willing to leave, for a few days at least.

Upstairs, I got out my laptop and brought up the file with my earlier notes. Some of them needed rethinking before I talked to Katy. A lot of rethinking.

I was reasonably sure I didn't need to worry about Cato anymore. Also, he knew the fight had been two against one so he didn't need my input. More importantly, Billy Joe could not have been one of the men involved. I'd seen the edge of the building, not a plane. There was no room to land a plane anyway if the property was bounded by an arroyo.

So what was the problem?

Katy, of course. Not the fight, not the sheriff, not the smuggling of Mexicans or drugs. Katy was my problem. We had been friends all our lives, I simply couldn't leave her here to face the situation, whatever it was, on her own, and I didn't know enough to talk her into leaving. Just telling her Billy Joe might be mixed up in something illegal wasn't going to do it. She wouldn't believe me to start with, and even if I had proof, she'd be far more likely to immediately face him and demand he stop whatever it was he was doing than she was to leave him.

I sat there for the next hour, weighing one fact against another, one educated guess against another, before I shut the computer off and started getting ready for the party.

The party, held in a huge private room at the club, was already in full swing when we arrived. Velma Jean met us at the door.

"Katy, Demary, you're here. I was beginning to think you weren't coming," she said with a welcoming smile.

If Velma Jean remembered my gaffe of the night before she certainly covered it well. She seemed glad to see me.

"We aren't late," Katy protested. She looked around at the already full room. "But we sure aren't early either, are we? Is Linda here yet?"

"She came about five minutes ago, and you will never believe the dress she has on. It's absolutely gorgeous. She looks like a million dollars."

Katy grinned but didn't reveal our part in getting Linda to buy and wear the dress. We both told Velma Jean she looked sensational as well.

Her dress, a floor-length peach-colored chiffon with layers of ruffles, reminded me of the outfits Ginger Rogers wore in the old movies. On anyone else the dress would have looked preposterous. Velma Jean looked like a Dresden Doll.

Three waitresses were circling through the room with trays of brimming champagne glasses. "Everyone take a glass," someone called out. "James is going to make a toast."

We all did as we were bid and after some milling around

found our places at the tables. James Hill stood up and raised his glass. He was just the man to make a toast. With his military bearing and look of distinction he commanded attention. He told a funny story about Leroy and Velma Jean's college courtship and everyone toasted the beaming couple.

Billy Joe followed James. His toast brought roars of laughter.

One more sentimental salute followed and then the waitresses started serving dinner. Again, a scrumptious meal: a succulent cut of prime rib of beef with a sour cream and horseradish sauce, baked potatoes with all the fixings, and Caesar salad with fresh gulf shrimp.

Another couple of days in Del Rio and I not only wouldn't be able to get my jeans zipped, my cholesterol count would hit the stratosphere.

After we finished eating, Velma Jean's planned seating was abandoned in favor of switching seats here and there to greet old friends or carry on a special conversation. Katy, easy to spot in her flame-colored satin jumpsuit, wandered from one table to another with a beaming Billy Joe in tow. As table-hopping didn't appeal to me at the moment—I was too full—I stayed where I was, drinking coffee and observing the other women's clothes.

It was definitely a dress-up party. My peacock blue shot-silk sheath was right on, especially as I had also worn my Mandel's necklace with its iridescent lamp-work beads. It compared more than favorably with the jeweled baubles in evidence on the other women.

Linda, sitting at a table to my right, looked stunning in her new dress. She was talking to Billy Joe's lawyer, Arnold Johnson. I had been introduced to him and his sister, Gladdie, much older than he, my first night in Del Rio.

Johnson, looking highly irritated—which surprised me, as lawyers usually manage not to show such expressions—was shaking his head at his sister when Linda suddenly lunged to her feet and slapped Gladdie across the face.

"How dare you say that," she cried, her voice rising easily above the general hubbub. "You don't even know Gerald."

The other woman was obviously too shocked to respond. She lifted a hand to her rapidly coloring cheek and stared at Linda with a horrified expression.

I stood up, but before I could move Katy appeared beside their table.

I couldn't hear what she said but in a moment she looked around, spotted me standing, and motioned me over.

"Please go with Linda," she said, her voice jerky with strain. "Take her to the ladies'. I'll be along in a minute. I want to talk to Gladdie."

"Forget it," Gladdie said. The imprint of Linda's hand was turning bright red. "I don't need talking to, but Linda certainly does."

The three of us got as far as the lobby, where Linda jerked her arm out of Katy's grasp and said she was going home.

"Oh, Linda. Please don't," Katy said. "Please try . . ."

Linda shook her head. "No, I can't, Katy. There's no use

in pretending any longer. Something has happened to Gerald. I'm going home where he, or the hospital, or whoever, can reach me. And regardless of what anybody says I'm going to call Frank tomorrow morning. Nobody around here seems to care what's happened to Gerald, but he will."

"Linda, we do care," Katy protested. "But Gerald's only been gone overnight. And we care about you too. You shouldn't be alone feeling the way . . ."

"I'll be alright." She whirled around and was out the door before Katy could say any more.

"Like she says, she'll be alright," Calvin Black drawled, startling us.

I had seen him out of the corner of my eye as we came out of the banquet room but hadn't realized he was still standing in the doorway to the bar.

Katy gave him a poisonous glare and went back to the party.

"What makes you say she'll be alright?" I asked neutrally. "Gerald has been gone quite a while. Did he . . ." I stopped in mid-sentence, covering my near-slip with a coughing fit. I had forgotten Cato's warning about talking to Calvin.

Calvin laughed, a humorless showing of teeth that gave his face a vulpine cast. "People with her kind of money always come out all right."

He slapped a big cream-colored Stetson on his head and strode out the door, snapping his fingers at the attendant to bring his car around.

Watching him walk down the stairs triggered a picture

memory in my mind's eye. An enormous fragment of the puzzle fell into place. Other bits and pieces were beginning to come together too. The big picture still eluded me, but some parts at least were getting clearer.

Chapter Twenty-One

W hen I returned to the party, the dining tables had been
replaced by small cocktail tables spotted around the edge
of a dance floor. A four-piece band had set up on a narrow
stage at the far side of the floor and was tuning up to play.

Katy waved to me from the nearby corner where Velma
Jean, Leroy, Billy Joe, and several others were crowded
around a lounge chair. Velma Jean, practically incandescent
with delight, was showing off the anniversary present
Leroy had just put on her finger.

"To the rousing cheers of everyone in the room," Katy
said, giving me a strained smile.

"I can see why," I said, nearly gasping at the size of the
diamond. The ring held a two-carat stone in a Tiffany setting surrounded by a collar of magnificent emeralds.

"I love it," Velma Jean chortled. She leaned across the

coffee table to plant a big kiss on Leroy's responsive mouth.

With all the goodwill floating around it seemed a shrewd time to launch my latest brainstorm.

After voicing more compliments and congratulations I turned a laughing face to Billy Joe.

"I'm trying to talk Katy into coming to Houston with me tomorrow. Maybe you'd better come with us or she'll decide she needs one of those on her finger too." I figured he couldn't object to her going with all his friends around.

General merriment greeted this sally. Then, to my dismay, Billy Joe said, "That's a great idea, Demary. I've been meaning to get over there soon anyway. We'll take the Mercedes to Midland in the morning and catch the two o'clock plane. Be in Houston in time for dinner at Pappadeaux's in the Galveston yacht harbor. Leroy? Velma Jean? How about you? Let's all make a weekend of it."

Before they could answer Katy stood up, knocking her chair over with a crash. Bright red streaks of color stained her cheekbones.

"I can't believe you, any of you," she said in a furious voice. "Linda is supposed to be our friend. She's worried sick about Gerald and not a one of you seems to give a darn. And now you want to walk off and abandon her here on her own."

"Whoa there, honey," Billy Joe said quickly. He picked up her chair and put his arm around her, gently forcing her to sit back down. "Nobody is going to desert Linda, honey. We'll take her with us. There's no need to get so worked up over Gerald's . . ."

Katy shot me an anguished look and before Billy Joe could stop her had wrenched herself out of his grasp and run out of the room. He followed, still trying to talk to her.

We all jumped to our feet. I told Velma Jean and Leroy to stay where they were. "After all, it's your party," I said with what I hoped was a reassuring smile. "Katy certainly doesn't want to spoil it for you. Let me go talk to her."

I hurried out in Billy Joe's wake. I found him standing in front of the door to the ladies' room, looking uncertain and extremely anxious.

"There's probably a whole bunch of women in there besides Katy," he said nervously. "I can't go charging in there after her."

"I should certainly hope not. Don't worry. I'll get her to calm down."

"You tell her to get out here. I want to talk to her."

"Billy Joe, didn't anyone ever tell you Lincoln freed the slaves?" I snapped, momentarily losing my cool. "You don't own her and I don't think she wants to talk to you at the moment, so go back to the party and leave her alone for a while." My nerves were twanging like banjo strings and I was fed up with macho males. Although, I could see that this one was a good deal more worried than he wanted to let on.

As it happened, Katy was the room's sole occupant, sitting on a velvet bench in front of one of the big mirrors. "Go away," she said angrily when she saw me behind her. "You're the worst of the lot. This sure teaches me not to ever count on you for any help."

Taking a deep breath, I reminded her that I had only

known Linda for three days. I had simply forgotten about her for a moment. Also, that I had no intention of deserting anyone, Linda included.

I sat down on the bench beside her and in a moment she reached over and squeezed my hand.

"I'm sorry, Demary. I didn't mean it. You know that. It's just that I've been worried sick ever since we found the car. And I can't figure out why Orin said not to tell Billy Joe. Demary, can't you find out what's going on? Does Cato think Billy Joe has something to do with Gerald's disappearance? If Billy Joe is mixed up in something bad I'll, I'll . . . I don't know what I'll do." Her face crumpled.

"Katy, don't you dare start crying," I snapped, giving her shoulder a hard shake. "Billy Joe is outside in the hall, and if you don't get out there and reassure him you're all right he's going to come apart. There's no sense in getting yourself into a snit, about him or anything else.

"Oh all right," I added as she continued to look teary-eyed. "I'll do what I can to find out about Gerald but you're going to have to straighten up and give me a hand."

"What? I'll do whatever you say," Katy said eagerly, her face lighting up. "You know how to do this kind of thing, Demary, you can . . ."

"Now wait a minute," I said quickly. "Don't get carried away. There's no guarantee I can do anything at all. Due to your big mouth," I made a face at her, "everyone here thinks I'm a PI. People won't want to talk to me."

"Tell me what you want to know. They'll talk to me, all right, or they'll be darn sorry they didn't. Who do I . . ."

"Nothing and nobody tonight. At the moment, all I want you to do is calm down," I told her. "And don't say anything about me or what I might do. Not even to Billy Joe. Agreed?"

"Yes. Okay. But why not Billy Joe? Do you think . . . ?" Her eyes were beginning to fill again.

"I don't think anything yet," I said quickly. "It's simply that the fewer people who pay any attention to me the better off I'll be."

Katy scowled, picking up on my train of thought and not liking it.

I got up and pulled her to her feet. Katy wasn't stupid. I didn't want her to do too much thinking. "Now, get. Go tell Billy Joe all is well."

She nodded. "Are you coming?"

"In a minute. Before you go, who is Frank and why is Linda going to call him?"

"He's her cousin. He's an assistant or something to the State Attorney General up in Santa Fe." She stopped with her hand on the door and looked back at me. "What are you going to do, Demary?"

"I haven't the faintest idea," I said, stalling. I urged her on out with a quick smile.

I had a very good idea of what I was going to do, or try to do.

Chapter Twenty-Two

Billy Joe was pacing the hall, looking harassed and truly unhappy. Katy flew into his arms. They stood for a moment clasped together and then he led her down the hall, murmuring in her ear.

It occurred to me—somewhat belatedly—that these two were still very much in love.

The party was in full swing. A number of the guests were taking advantage of the dance floor. Leroy grabbed me as I came in the door and whirled me out into the center of it with a double spin. He was a virtuoso dancer, smooth and expert. I'm no slouch myself. The band played a fast three-piece set which kept both of us on our toes. It was great fun. We finished up on the far side of the room from where we started, slightly breathless and full of conceit at our proficiency.

"That was quite a performance, Demary," Leroy said,

beaming at me. "Where did you pick up that double clog step?"

One of my few athletic accomplishments is ballroom dancing and I am good. I demonstrated the clog step for him and we started back across the room in high good humor.

As we neared the doorway I asked if he'd mind stepping out in the hall for just a moment. I really was sorry to disrupt our camaraderie, but knew I'd never have a better chance to talk to him.

He looked surprised, and slightly flustered, but he followed me out the door. I wondered, amused, if he thought I was going to come on to him.

I led him a couple of steps away from the door, decided there was no way of camouflaging the question, and asked him straight out if he'd tell me exactly what happened on Monday night when he and Billy Joe landed at the municipal airport.

For a second, I thought he was going to refuse, but then he changed his mind. His pale hazel eyes darkened with some emotion I couldn't define.

"It wasn't night, it hadn't even started to get dark yet." he said. "We landed at four-twenty. You can check the log if you like. Billy Joe taxied up to the hangar, we talked to the mechanic, checked into the office, and went home."

"Together?"

Leroy fixed me with a penetrating look. "What's your interest in what we did?" he asked.

"Nothing sinister," I assured him. "I'm simply trying to

get a line on where Gerald's gone. I know he saw Billy Joe that afternoon and I wondered if it was at the airport." I didn't know anything of the kind. I was guessing, but it was an educated guess.

Leroy pursed his mouth, no doubt deciding what or how much to tell me. It didn't matter now. His attitude had already told me what I wanted to know.

"Yes, he met us at the field," he said finally. "Or I guess I should say he met Billy Joe. He came running across the tarmac the minute we came to a stop and hustled Billy Joe off around the side of the hangar. In a few minutes Billy Joe came back, asked me to finish up with the plane and they left. I didn't see either one of them again until dinner that night. Here."

"Let's go dance up another storm," I said, giving him a brilliant smile.

"That's all you wanted to know?" He sounded so disappointed I had to laugh. I couldn't imagine what he'd expected.

"That's it," I said.

The band was playing an old-fashioned jitterbug, and dance up a storm we did. We finished the set to a round of laughter and cheers.

"You've been holding out on us, Leroy," a woman in a sequined mini-dress called out. "Velma Jean, how come you don't do that stuff?"

"What do you mean, I don't do that stuff? C'mon, lover, let's show the peasants how it's really done," Velma Jean retorted.

She grabbed Leroy around the neck, signaled to the band and the two of them swung into a incredible exhibition of the Argentine tango.

I meant to fade into the background since I had someone else I wanted to talk to, but they were so great I stayed glued in position until the end. They finished to an absolute riot of applause.

Katy and Billy Joe returned sometime during the fun and took to the floor as well.

Later in the evening, through a break in the crowd, I saw Billy Joe in close conversation with Arnold Johnson, the attorney, and to judge by their body language neither one was enjoying what the other had to say. Billy Joe had a three-corner rip in his shirt sleeve that fluttered like an agitated moth as he gestured at the lawyer.

It took me a little time, but I finally maneuvered myself into a position where James Hill asked me to dance. The straightforward approach had worked out all right with Leroy so I decided to try it again. We were dancing a fancy slow dance when I asked him what his truck had been doing in the yard the night before and who the men getting in the back had been.

"Just a couple of boys from down around Sonora. They been working for Billy Joe this summer," he answered absently, twirling me around another couple. "I gave them a ride home, or at least as far as Van Horn. I had a load to pick up down there. They can make their own way over the border from there. Why?"

"Just curious."

He nodded, unconcerned, and spun me around in the opposite direction.

There were a lot of really good dancers in this group.

The party started breaking up shortly after two in the morning. We were among the last to leave, so it was close to three when we arrived home.

Sheet lightning flickered along the horizon as Billy Joe let Katy and me out in front of the house. He wanted to take a quick run down to the stables to check on one of his mares that was due to foal.

"I'll be back in a couple of minutes," he said, leaning out the car window. "How about putting some coffee on? By the time it's done I'll be back and we can scramble up some eggs. Okay?"

We agreed. Scrambled eggs sounded great.

In the kitchen I asked Katy if she had ever heard of the Penniwait place.

"Of course," she said, setting out plates and silverware. "Their north boundary runs along our south section."

That answered the question of why Gary was working on the Valentine ranch. "Did you know they were having some kind of a standoff down there with the feds?"

"Over a bunch of illegals? Sure. I haven't paid much attention though."

"You never mentioned it."

She got out the coffee and started measuring grounds into the filter basket. "Why should I?" she asked, frowning at me. "It doesn't amount to much. Ridiculous, really. Why are you interested, anyway?"

"Smuggling illegals into the country and using them as slaves doesn't sound ridiculous to me," I said, somewhat sharply. "It sounds appalling."

"Doing what? Where in the world did you hear that, Demary?"

I repeated what the waitress down south had said.

"She didn't know what she was talking about. I told you before, everyone around here hires illegals. Crystle always has at least two girls working for her who don't have green cards. So does Velma Jean. All the ranchers hire them. They need the money and we need the help. For one thing, they're hard workers. Half the regular hands you hire won't do a darn thing if you're not watching them every minute."

"And I don't imagine it hurts any that they'll work for anything you want to pay them."

Katy laughed. "What century are you living in, Demary? Maybe that's the way it was fifty years ago but it sure as heck isn't that way now. Just because they don't speak good English doesn't mean they're stupid. They know what the going wage is and that's what they get paid. They work six or eight months and then go back to their families. Sometimes they go home for a month or so and then come back. They are good people."

Her patronizing tone ticked me off, especially as she didn't know what she was talking about. The INS doesn't send in an undercover agent to investigate a couple of housemaids who don't have work permits.

However, this wasn't a good time to be getting into an argument on the question of illegal immigrants. I was sorry now that I'd brought it up. Billy Joe would be back any moment.

I switched the conversation to Leroy and Velma Jean and her new ring, clog-stepping around the table as I put out the napkins.

Chapter Twenty-Three

W hen I came downstairs at eleven-thirty the next morning Katy was still in her pajamas, lying on a patio lounge
chair and drinking a cup of coffee.

"About time you got up," she said, smiling. Her silky
dark blond hair shone in the sunlight. She covered a yawn
with pink-tipped fingers. "Wasn't last night fun?"

"Uh-huh." I poured myself a cup of coffee from the carafe on the side table, thinking that last night might have
been fun but here we were, still in Del Rio, and with no
plans to leave.

"Where's Billy Joe?" I asked.

She glanced at her watch. "He just went in to call Linda
and invite her over for brunch. Carmella is fixing it now.
Billy Joe still thinks he can persuade her to . . ." She sat up
with a jerk. "Billy Joe? What's the matter?"

Billy Joe had appeared in the doorway. He stood there

for a second, straightened his shoulders, and moved quickly to Katy's side. His normally ruddy complexioned face had a gray cast.

"Katy, I . . . I don't know how . . ."

"What?" Katy's eyes widened with fear. "What? What's wrong?"

"Linda," he said hoarsely. "Orin was there when I called. He just found her. She's dead, Katy. She . . ." He swallowed, unable to go on.

Katy turned chalk-white. "What happened?" she whispered, her eyes wide with shock.

Billy Joe shook his head.

"What happened to her?" Katy repeated, her voice climbing. She reached over to set her coffee cup on the edge of the planter. She missed. It fell to the tiles, splintering into shards. Neither one of them noticed.

Billy Joe knelt down in front of her and took her hands in his. "Orin went over to her place this morning to talk to her about Gerald. He found the door ajar. She was lying on the floor in the hall, and . . . I don't think you want to know any more than that, Katy," he said, looking over at me for support. He didn't get it.

Katy was a lot tougher than he thought. Her fingers dug into the back of his hand. "What happened to her?" she demanded. "What did Orin say? Tell me, right now!"

Billy Joe started to speak, checked himself, then went on in a flat, matter-of-fact tone. "She was still wearing the dress she had on at the party, so it must have happened not long after she got home. She probably opened the door for whoever it was, there was no sign of forced entry, and it looks like he . . . he hit her . . . hard, knocked her out, and . . . and then he broke her neck. Orin has put out a state-wide APB for Gerald," he finished.

"What?" Katy's voice rose sharply, and I wondered if Billy Joe saw the danger signals. Maybe he'd never seen Katy when she got a head of steam up. "What? He thinks Gerald killed her? Is he crazy? Gerald adored her! He would no more kill her than . . . than . . ." She choked off the rest of the sentence and stood up, wrenching herself away from Billy Joe's restraining hand.

"Damn you, all of you. If you'd paid any attention to her, tried to help her she . . . she . . . Demary, get your things packed. We're leaving." She whipped around and started for the door. "But first we're going into town and talk to Orin. I have a few things to say to that b—" She deleted the rest.

Billy Joe made a mistake. They'd been married two years, he should have known better. "Katy, don't be silly. You can't do that," he said, taking several fast steps toward her. He grabbed her wrist, pulling her around toward him.

She looked down at his hand. "Take your hand off my arm," she said slowly, spacing every word out separately. "And don't try to tell me what I can or cannot do. I'll do anything I darn well please. And I wouldn't try to stop me if I were you."

The back of Billy Joe's neck turned dark red. He jerked his hand away, favored both of us with a stony glance and strode out of the room.

"Uh, you came on a little strong there, didn't you?" I said in a prosaic tone.

"Strong?" She spoke in the same carefully controlled voice, rage simmering just below the surface. "I wasn't half strong enough. If he, or the rest of them had paid any attention to Linda, if that fatherless s.o.b. Orin Cato had done his job to start with, Linda wouldn't be dead." Tears ran down her face. She brushed them away angrily.

"I'm leaving now, right now, as soon as I can throw a change of clothes into a bag. And I don't know when I'll be back. I don't know if I'll ever want to see any of these people again. Maybe I never will! Are you coming?"

"I'll meet you in the hall. Ten minutes."

She nodded and disappeared up the stairs.

I didn't bother packing. I knew Katy. She could change her mind faster than I could change clothes. I put on clean jeans, a Seahawks T-shirt, and sneakers, shoved my toothbrush in my pocket, and was ready to go.

Katy came in as I started for the door. "Try your telephone," she said brusquely, turning the key in the door behind her.

There was no dial tone.

"None of the phones are working," she said, her eyes glittering with fury. "If he thinks he can . . ."

"Whoa. Hold on, Katy. How do you know Billy Joe had anything to do with it? The lines just may be down somewhere."

"Bull cookies! My car won't start and I'll give you ten to one yours won't either."

Katy was right.

We stood in the shadow of the shed and tried to decide

what to do next. Katy was so angry she practically shot sparks.

"Isn't there a pickup here somewhere?" I asked. "I thought I saw one of the men driving one with Valentine Ranch painted on the side."

"Yes, but I doubt if it's around at this time of day. The men are usually using it to haul hay or something. It'll be down by the barn if no one has it out. C'mon. We'll look."

"Wait a minute, Katy." I laid a restraining hand on her arm. "Let me think this through. Somebody, and we don't know that it's Billy Joe, has disabled both our cars and the telephone. He, or she, has gone to some trouble to keep us here, so I'm not sure the pickup is a good idea after all. I think maybe we'd be better off walking." Katy started to interrupt but I shushed her and went on.

"Leroy told me the other night that a person on foot is almost impossible to spot from any distance. It's only a few miles into town. If we stay off the road there's less chance of our being seen. We could be there in an hour, maybe less. As soon as we see some place with a phone I'll call Carol Ann and she can come charging to the rescue." I didn't tell her I was wishing I had my cell phone along to call Carol Ann right then. I had a creepy feeling that someone was watching us and would have given a lot for some back up.

"It's seven miles into town," Katy said bluntly. "And it must be ninety out already. We'd be dead of sunstroke before we were halfway there."

She was right. Again.

"You do ride, don't you?" she asked, a sudden gleam in her eyes. "I can't remember."

"A horse, you mean?"

"Yes, of course I mean a horse."

"Yes, I can ride. Better than I play golf."

"Then let's go. If the pickup is in the barn we'll take it and chance someone trying to stop us, but if not we'll saddle a couple of horses and head for the Hills' place. Their house is less than five miles cross country. We should have Stetsons to protect us from the sun but we can make do with straw hats. There's always a couple of them in the tack room."

"Can you saddle a horse?" I couldn't envision her doing any such thing.

"You'd be surprised what I can do," she said, favoring me with a wicked grin.

Some twenty minutes later, we rode two of James Hill's appaloosas out of the stable and headed north toward their home ranch. In the best movie tradition, we stayed off the road and kept the line of elms around the house between us and any prying eyes until we were well away. Ahead of us lay flat, skimmed-off rangeland, holding neither friend nor foe, nor, as far as I could see, anything else either. There were no oil rigs in this direction, nor any fences. Nothing but shimmering heat waves.

Chapter Twenty-Four

W hen I assured Katy I could ride I told the truth. I could ride better than I played golf, but considering my golf game, that wasn't saying much. What I should have said was that with luck I could stay on a horse. Fortunately these two were well-mannered and used to being ridden together. The one I rode followed slightly behind and to one side of his mate in a steady trot that took us well out of sight of the house within a few minutes.

The sun was directly overhead and very, very hot.

"Katy, do you know what the heck you're doing?" I asked crossly. She had been crying steadily ever since we left the stable.

She didn't answer and we continued to ride.

Some time later I saw what appeared to be trees ahead of us, hopefully on the outskirts of the Hills' ranch.

They were not. They surrounded a small broken-down

building, a stack of hay bales, and a dilapidated old flatbed wagon with one wheel missing. The trees had already shed some of their leaves, but even so it was considerably cooler in their shade than out in the open.

I dismounted, tied my horse, who was named Petey, to a low-hanging branch and sat down on the side of the wagon to mop my face and neck with a tissue.

Katy watched me dismally for a moment, then did the same.

"This heat is not doing me or my disposition any good," I said, resisting a desire to shake her. "And if you don't straighten up and talk to me I'm going to . . ." I looked around. The arid, unchanging terrain flowed relentlessly toward the horizon in all directions. Leroy was right about one thing. It was impossible to see any distance in this flat country.

"I don't know what I'm going to do," I admitted. "But I wish you'd quit that whimpering and tell me . . ."

"I'm not whimpering," Katy wailed.

I put my arm around her and gave her a hug. "All right, Katy. You're not whimpering. You're crying for Linda, I know that. But we've got to decide what we're going to do. We can't wander around out here all day."

"I just can't quit crying," she said, hiccuping. "Linda was my first friend here, my only friend at first. Crystle was hateful and all the rest, even Velma Jean, were so standoffish. Linda was the only one who even tried to be nice. I just can't believe Gerald would kill her."

"He didn't. At least I don't think he did."

She mopped her wet face with her sleeve. "But who . . . ?"

"The same person who killed Gary."

Her tears ceased abruptly. "Gary? What did he have to do with Linda? I don't think she ever even saw him."

I took Larry Morrison's ID folder out of my hip pocket and handed it to her. I'd remembered it that morning, remembered finding it on the walk in front of the house when we came back from the club the first night I'd been in Del Rio. It had still been in the pocket of my dress. I hadn't known at the time that it was Larry Morrison's; I'd thought it was Billy Joe's. I only found out who it belonged to when it fell on the floor an hour ago as I was jerking clothes out of my bag looking for a shirt.

Katy stared at it with an uncomprehending expression. "I don't understand," she said slowly. "What was he doing here? The INS surely wasn't investigating us. The few Mexicans we have around the place might get us a fine if the border patrol caught them, but a federal man? That's crazy. And what would he have to do with Linda?"

"I don't know," I said truthfully. "But I do know illegals have something to do with what has been going on around here." I told her what I'd seen out by the barn: the men getting into the cattle truck.

"But James was just giving them a ride home," Katy protested, frowning at me. "What's so wrong about that?"

I sighed. "Nothing, I guess. I don't know. What I am sure of is that Gerald knew him. Knew Gary." I stopped and thought. "No, that might not be right. But Gerald knew something about his death, maybe he was there, saw what happened. And he may have told Linda. That's why he was killed and why Linda was killed."

She slid off the wagon and stood facing me, frowning. "He's dead? Gerald's dead? Killed? How do you know? And who did it? Who killed them?"

I shook my head. "I'm not sure. The only people I'm reasonably certain didn't kill Gary are Billy Joe and Leroy, and to tell the truth, I'm not all that darn positive about them. Their alibi, such as it is, isn't that ironclad. But they do know about what's going on. That I'm sure of."

"Billy Joe kill somebody? You must be out of your mind."

"How did he get that tear in his shirt last night?"

"How did he . . . ?" For a second her eyes blazed with anger, then suddenly she snickered. "Well, he didn't get it strangling Linda, I can assure you of that," she said.

"Oh," I said, feeling both embarrassed and stupid as I recalled them going off down the clubhouse hallway with their arms around each other.

"Gary must have been here because of what's going on down at the Penniwait place, wasn't he?" Katy asked.

"Probably."

She stared at the ground, her face closed in and thoughtful. In a few moments she came out of her reverie and started over to untie the horses.

"Let's go back," she said, reaching for the reins.

"No, not yet. Sit down here and let me tell you what I think must have happened."

I started at the beginning with the fight in the gravel yard, and told her what I'd seen and heard and deduced. She didn't like it, as I'd known she wouldn't, but she didn't interrupt or argue.

When I got to the end, Linda's death, the tears started again. I sat and waited, sweat trickling down my back and under my arms.

It was peaceful and still under the trees. The horses made soft snuffling sounds as they cropped the dry grass. I could hear the sound of a plane in the far distance.

"What do you want to do?" she asked finally, taking a deep breath.

"Katy, somebody cut the phone lines and disabled both our cars. I don't know why but I sure don't think it was meant to be a joke. I want to do what I said to start with. Get to town and talk to Carol Ann first, then find the sheriff, or whoever. Even though she isn't local, once Carol Ann knows the whole story we're safe."

Nodding in agreement, Katy untied the two horses, mounted, and handed me my reins. I pulled the animal over to the wagon. I couldn't get aboard without standing on something, he was too tall.

As I stepped up on the sideboard I lost my balance and fell to my knees on the wagon bed. I let out a yelp and dropped my reins. I'd hit my funny bone as I fell. Petey danced sideways, eyeing me dubiously. I slid back to the ground and reached for the reins again but he moved away from me, his head tilted warily. The reins trailed down one side of his neck.

"Stand still," Katy said quickly. "You've scared him. Stay still until I can catch him." She nudged her animal into a slow walk. My mount backed some more. Talking in a soft soothing tone, she kept moving slowly toward the now nervous Petey. He didn't like the reins hanging around his legs and tossed his head from side to side in irritation. Suddenly he whirled and headed for the open prairie, caramel-colored mane flying.

Katy, showing considerably more horse expertise than I had any idea she possessed, kicked her own animal into a run and went after my fast-disappearing gelding. A minute later I was completely alone. Nothing, or nobody, but my own miserable sweat-soaked self was visible in any direction.

Chapter Twenty-Five

I sat watching the opening between the trees where Katy had disappeared and hoped she could find her way back to me, with or without Petey.

Time passed.

I began to seriously wonder if I'd ever see Katy again, or Seattle, or civilization.

More time passed.

I got hotter, I got thirstier, my T-shirt was sticking to my back and my front, and I began to worry. I would hate to have to walk back to the Valentine ranch. Particularly so because I had no idea where the ranch was. Fortunately, about that time Katy showed on the horizon, two moving spots between the trees.

"Stupid animal," she fumed as she rode up. "Running off like that. I never would have caught him if he hadn't got tangled in a mesquite, and then the silly thing wouldn't let

162

me near him to set him free. That mesquite had two-inch thorns. Look at the scratches he got. James will have a conniption fit. He's James's favorite parade horse."

"How did you ever find your way back to me?"

"I was only just a little way over there. I could see the trees. If you'd stood up you could have seen me. Here." She handed me Petey's reins.

I reached to take them but Petey sidled away skittishly.

"Maybe I'd better change with you. You ride Jocko here and I'll . . ." Katy started to say.

I jumped down, grabbed the reins out of her hand, jerked Petey over to the wagon, and climbed into the saddle. Petey sidestepped in a half circle. I wrenched his head back around, gave him a sharp kick in the ribs, and rode out of the trees. I was in no mood to cater to a blasted horse. Petey got the message and decided to behave.

"Which way are we going?" I asked surveying our surroundings, which consisted mainly of mesquite and tumbleweed. There didn't seem to be any signposts.

Katy peered skyward, searched the horizon, and moved out on what she said was a westerly course. She said Del Rio should be in that direction and if we had wandered too far north we would at least hit the main highway within a mile or so.

I checked my watch. It was exactly 2:45.

At 3:20 we stopped, stood in our stirrups, and searched for signs of . . . anything. I saw a lot of mesquite, tumbleweed, some beaver-tail cactus, and three cows. Nothing else. There wasn't even a fence in sight.

"I think we're going in circles," I said, looking at Katy uneasily. "Where did all this empty land come from, anyway? We haven't even seen an oil rig road. It's like we dropped off the end of the world."

Katy took a swallow from her canteen. I'd made fun of her, saying she'd been watching too many old movies when she insisted on filling two before we set out, but both of us were thankful we had them now.

"I think we must have passed east of the Hills' place without my noticing," she decided. "We're probably too far north and east now. We must have got over onto the State Conservation Reserve. We better backtrack south a little."

She pulled Jocko to her left and gave him a nudge. He balked, reared up on his hind legs, and Katy slid off his rump. We were both using English saddles—the only kind she knew how to rig—little flat pieces of leather that weren't a whole lot better than riding bareback. Jocko stepped around her in a complete circle, tossing his head fretfully. She did have sense enough to hang on to his reins. Better than I had done.

Swearing in what I took to be some Scandinavian dialect, she remounted and we set off again.

A little later, pulling up my collar to cover my neck, it suddenly dawned on me that if we were riding southwest the sun should be in my eyes, not burning the back of my neck.

I jerked Petey to a stop. "Katy, do you have any idea at all where we are?" I demanded.

She came to a stop, mopping her face with the tail of her shirt. "Not the slightest," she admitted. "But if we keep going west we are bound to find . . ."

"Then we better start going in the right direction," I yelled. "We're riding east!"

"How do you know?" Katy said peevishly. "You don't know anything about this country."

"I know enough to know the sun sets in the west," I snapped.

Katy looked at the sky.

I think I would have cried if I could have spared the moisture.

Again standing in the stirrups to peer around, I spotted a tall, dark clump of something behind us and to our right—which, if the sun hadn't changed orbit, should have been south. "If we've been going in circles that might be the same bunch of trees we found before," I said, pointing.

"It can't be."

But it was. The same trees, the same broken-down house, pile of hay, and dilapidated wagon. There was also a distinct set of tire tracks leading to and from the house. They were very faint—the ground was rock hard—and on the opposite side of where we had approached the place before, which was why hadn't seen them. Nor were they all that easy to see even as we crossed them coming in this second time.

Katy was the first to spot the tread imprints and turned Jocko. "Look," she cried. "Tire tracks. They must lead to a road. We can follow them."

"No. Wait. Katy, I've got to get out of this sun for a few minutes. I'm getting lightheaded. Let me go lay down on that wagon bed for a little bit, then we can follow the tracks to town."

Katy agreed. She didn't look too good herself. "Darn! Why didn't we see them before?"

"We were over on the other side. I wonder if there's a well or something near the house. There must be water around here somewhere or these trees wouldn't be here. My canteen's dry and I'm beginning to feel pretty rocky from dehydration."

"I'll go see."

She hopped off Jocko and went looking. "The house is padlocked," she called. "Strange, it's a new padlock but there's nothing inside except a table and a big plastic bag laying on the floor. I can see it through the window. There's no sink or pump. Whoever was staying here may have packed their water in, but still, there should be a well."

I lay flat on the wagon bed trying to summon some strength. Redheads do not do well in hot climates. At least, I don't. The sun can really lay me out. I could hear Katy still talking on the far side of the clearing but I couldn't make out the words.

I closed my eyes. I was almost dozing when what she'd said drifted back into my mind.

A new padlock on an abandoned building? Empty except for a plastic bag?

"Katy, where are you? Come here a minute," I called.

She came around the side of the hay. "You ready to go?"

"No. That plastic bag you saw. In the house. How big was it?"

She shrugged. "Pretty big. A big black one. It's got something in it or I don't suppose whoever it belongs to would have bothered padlocking the door. But I couldn't tell what it was. Seemed kind of puffed up."

I slid off the wagon and walked over to the house with Katy trailing in my wake. In addition to being dizzy, my stomach was now tying itself in knots.

One look in the window confirmed my guess. The sack was a body bag. The kind the police or the coroner's office use to transport a corpse. And I'd be willing to bet my last dollar there was a corpse inside this one too. Gerald Cameron's corpse. Not only that, there was an open attaché case that seemed to be at least partly smashed on the floor under the table. Several plastic bags filled with a white powder were visible inside. I remembered the woman with her arm chopped off and cocaine dust in her hair. If she had been carrying the attaché case when she walked into the prop of the plane it would explain the condition of the case and the cocaine on her hair and clothes. Maybe, maybe not. At any rate, I was reasonably sure the bags weren't full of powdered sugar. Not hidden out here in this desolate place beside a body bag.

Chapter Twenty-Six

I told Katy what I thought was in the bags.

"Are you going to look and see?" she asked in a whisper.

"Not in this lifetime."

"We have to know," she said. He voice sounded strange without its usual vivacity.

"Katy! If that is Gerald's body in there it's been there since Tuesday sometime. Those bags are typically airtight, and as Leroy said, it's been a warmish few days. He's been cooking in that thing, and at this point who cares what's in the little case."

Katy's face turned an interesting grey-green color. She ran around the side of the house, and I could hear her retching. I leaned on the building, my stomach cramping in sympathy. After a bit she came back and we wobbled over to sit on the edge of the wagon.

"I'm not positive, but I think I know where we are," Katy

168

said after a while, her voice still sick and shaky. "I'm pretty sure I was out here once with Billy Joe. I should've remembered before but . . ." She took in a deep breath. "If I'm right, this place is on the boundary line between our place and the Hills' place. The northeast corner. We're in Texas really."

"How far from town? Do you know?"

She frowned, thinking. "Eight, maybe nine miles. No more than that."

"If that's all, we should be able to see the glow from the lights in town as soon as the sun goes down. We can head for them, or we can follow the tracks back now. Follow them until we see a house anyway." I said. I felt significantly better now that I had some idea of where we were. "How did you and Billy Joe get out here? Horseback or . . ." I stopped to listen, thinking I'd heard a motor. In a moment I was sure. A car or truck was coming our way.

Katy heard it too and jumped to her feet. "Someone's coming. It sounds like the truck." She began running toward the far side of the trees where we'd seen the tire tracks.

"No, wait," I yelled, starting after her. "We don't know who it is."

She either didn't hear me or didn't care and I was miles too far behind to stop her. She had already run out from under the trees and was waving frantically at the oncoming pickup.

It came to a stop in a cloud of dust.

"What in the world are you two doing out here?" Calvin asked, leaning out the truck window with a big white-toothed grin.

Katy was right, he could manage to make a simple question sound like a loaded suggestion.

"We got lost," Katy said sharply, moving away from the truck. "But we're fine now. What are you doing out here yourself?"

I wished she hadn't said that. At least she didn't blurt out what we'd seen in the house, nor ask for a lift. I should have told her more but it was too late now.

"We've been for a ride," I said brightly, strolling forward to stand beside her. "We told Billy Joe we wouldn't be long but this is such a pretty spot we've been lolling around in the shade gossiping." I glanced at my watch. "And if we don't get a move on Billy Joe is going to be out here after us. He's such a worry-wart when it comes to Katy."

Forcing a smile, I gave her arm a surreptitious jerk and started backing up toward the horses.

Calvin shifted the truck into low and drove in under the trees beside the two animals, revving the motor as he did. Frightened, both horses reared, pulling back on their reins.

Katy jumped and grabbed their halters, one in each hand.

"What's the matter with you, Calvin?" she yelled. "Do you want them to bolt and leave us stranded out here?"

"Oh, I won't let anything like that happen," he said, laughing as he opened the door and got out. "I'll see that you're taken care of."

"I don't need you taking care of me, now or any other time," she snapped. "You . . ."

She broke off with a gasp as Calvin reached over and stroked her cheek. With both hands on the horses she was, for a moment, defenseless. But not for long. Before I could even move she let go of the halters and swung at him.

It was a respectable try—her brothers had taught her well—but Calvin was expecting it. He grabbed her hands in his and bent to kiss her.

The next several minutes were chaotic.

The horses reared and plunged around us as Katy twisted her face away from his mouth and brought her knee up into his belly in a fast reflex motion that caught him unawares. He let go of her hands and grabbed a handful of her hair. Katy screamed, frightening the horses even more.

I flung myself at Calvin in a rugby tackle, fingers clawing at his face.

Katy's right fist hit him square on the nose. Blood spurted like a fountain, all over him and all over me. His white shirt turned a brilliant red.

Bellowing with shock and anger, Calvin grabbed Katy by the arm and threw her six feet across the clearing. Whirling, he hit me with a backhand that knocked me silly and sent me skidding into the side of the wagon.

Swearing furiously, Calvin strode over and aimed a kick at Katy's ribs. She rolled away, taking his boot on her thigh, but his second kick caught the side of her jaw and she collapsed against the base of a tree.

I grabbed a rock and staggered to my feet. My intention was to batter him to a pulp—or at least try to—but fortunately I came to my senses and dropped the rock before I had done more than take a couple of steps.

"You've killed her," I gasped.

He glared at me. "She had it coming," he snarled. "She and that other bitch with their noses in the air. Think they're better than anyone else. Me and Billy Joe don't need them."

It was such a feeble motive for murder and I was so groggy I did the one thing I shouldn't have done. I screamed at him.

"Billy Joe will kill you if you hurt Katy," I screeched.

"Oh no he won't," he yelled. "He'll be glad to be rid of her. The same as that stupid Linda. Talking about her cousin going to the attorney general. I showed her! I'm the chief of police. I don't have to listen to the likes of her."

"Just like you showed Gary," I said, forcing myself to calm down, trying to sound as if killing Gary had been the sensible thing to do. It had finally sunk through my still fuzzy head that Calvin had slipped his moorings.

I could see Katy stirring. If we were to have any chance of staying alive it was going to take both of us. I had to keep him talking to me, facing me long enough for her to get to her feet. I didn't want to die in Texas.

"I showed him all right," he said, still glaring at me. Blood continued to drip from his nose in a steady stream but he didn't seem to notice. "That stupid Gerald tried to stop me using the pipe. Said just to 'talk' to him. Said he'd have to tell Orin but I put a stop to that. To both of them."

"Why'd you do it?" I asked, trying for a conversational tone. "Gary didn't amount to much. He couldn't have bothered you."

"He asked too many questions. Like you. I told him I'd throw him in the tank with a couple of hardcases to take care of him but he wouldn't listen. Just like you." He gave me a prurient smile. "Those same boys are going to love having you for a playmate for a few hours. But first I'm going to have me a little fun," he said, reaching for me.

Nobody could ever say Katy was a coward. Slowly, carefully, she had struggled to her feet, and now, reverting to some far-distant Viking ancestor, she tore into Calvin with a banshee howl that would have stopped a tank.

He sensed her coming but he wasn't fast enough. He turned just in time to meet her charge square on as she drove her head into his solar plexus. I launched myself from a sprinter's crouch and planted my rock behind his ear with the strength of desperation.

As the saying goes, he went down like a poleaxed steer.

The horses tore loose from their ties and galloped off across the prairie, neighing shrilly.

I had one single thought: get away before he wakes up enough to remember the gun strapped to his waist. I was too scared to try to take it off him. Grabbing each other for support, we ran for the truck, and with Katy driving we roared off behind the two horses.

Calvin was still stretched out on the ground.

Chapter Twenty-Seven

The yard was full of cars, people, and horses when, following the tracks in the dirt to the road, we screeched to a stop in front of Katy's house some fifteen minutes later. Billy Joe, James Hill, and Sheriff Cato stood on the steps as if waiting for us to arrive. Actually, they were talking to the search party assembled to search for us when Billy Joe discovered both cars disabled and the horses gone. The cars, as we found later, were Calvin's doing, although we never did discover what he had in mind. The dead phones were simply a bad coincidence. An eighteen-wheeler had swerved to avoid a cow standing in the middle of the highway and had hit a telephone pole.

Katy's slam-bang stop killed the motor, which was just as well as she practically fell out her door and ran for the comfort of Billy Joe's arms.

I just sat, my head resting against the window frame. I

174

was not only exhausted, I was beginning to suffer—and I use the word intentionally—from the effects of too much sun on bare skin. The backs of my hands were turning a fiery red and although I couldn't see my neck I could feel it and I knew it was the same color. Even my face, protected as it had been by the straw hat, felt hot and painful. I had a class-A sunburn. A fitting finale to a rotten day.

Two hours later, liberally coated with aloe pulp to quell the pain of my blistered neck, hands, and face, I snuggled down on my bed to—on the orders of the doctor Billy Joe had insisted on calling—sleep away the effects of what he called heat exhaustion.

The sheriff's men had left to collect Calvin, the body bag, and the attaché case, but again at the doctor's insistence, the sheriff had asked Katy and me very little beyond directions, saying he would be back that evening to talk to us.

I went to sleep comforted by the sure knowledge that the only thing Billy Joe had been guilty of was trying to protect Katy. Both his and Sheriff Cato's behavior had made that very clear.

That evening, feeling considerably better, I joined Billy Joe, Katy, and Sheriff Cato on the patio after a dinner tray in my room. I was not, however, feeling too pleased at being "summoned" to the meeting. The males of Del Rio, even if they wore a star, were beginning to fret me almost as bad as the heat.

"You were quite right," Cato said gravely after Billy Joe told me the body bag had contained Gerald's body. "It was Gerald. A terrible thing."

I wasn't sure whether he meant the murder itself or the condition of the body. I didn't ask. I asked instead, "Where was Calvin when your men got out to the place? Was he still there?"

He hesitated, obviously deciding how much he wanted to say.

"You might as well tell her what she wants to know," Billy Joe said with an amused grimace. "She'll worm it out of you one way or another."

I had a feeling Billy Joe thought me a bad influence on his wife.

The sheriff hemmed and hawed but finally revealed that Calvin had been digging a grave when the deputies arrived. He had not put up any resistance and had been handcuffed and taken to jail without any trouble. He had not even asked why he was being arrested.

Apparently, Calvin had lost all contact with reality.

"Did he tell you why he killed Gary? I mean, what was Gary asking questions about that set him off?" I asked Cato. "Was Calvin involved somehow with the standoff at the Penniwait ranch?"

"No. Not at all," he said in a resigned tone, sounding like Sam when he gave up and told me whatever I wanted to know. "And the Penniwait situation is no longer a standoff. It has been resolved satisfactorily and in good order."

"Resolved satisfactorily? What does that mean?" I demanded, hoping he didn't mean a Branch Dividian type ending.

The sheriff pulled on his lip, eyeing the drink in his hand as if he suspected it of being tainted. "The ah . . . the group inside simply walked out. They had arranged to have several lawyers present and . . . ah . . . that was all there was to it."

I grinned, glad to hear some of the "group inside" had the good sense to call in legal reinforcements. "Did Calvin even know about the Penniwait situation?"

Cato shook his head. "I doubt it. Calvin's election to his job was a piece of politicking that some people should be ashamed of," he added with a severe glance at Billy Joe, who had the grace to look embarrassed. "Calvin knew nothing about law enforcement and made no attempt to learn, so he wasn't involved in anything the rest of his office could reasonably keep him out of."

"Gary was asking questions about him around a couple of bars in town," Billy Joe said. "He must have heard something, probably from one of the hands, that gave him the idea Calvin did know about the Penniwait situation. But why that should have bothered Calvin I don't know."

"At least that's what Gerald told me. He met me at the airport when Leroy and I came back from Lubbock Monday. He was in a panic. Calvin had persuaded him to help him, as Calvin put it, 'give that snoopy hand a talking to that would teach him to keep his nose out of our business.' He said, Gerald I mean, said he went along with Calvin to try to keep him in line. I don't know how they got Gary to go out to the gravel storage with them but when the 'talking to' turned into a beating and with Gary dead, Gerald knew he'd be charged with being an accessory at the very least. He claimed he'd tried to stop Calvin using the pipe but that wouldn't help him any. Neither one of them had any idea Gary was an INS agent, nor did I until later."

"How did you find out?" I asked.

Billy Joe shrugged, looking faintly embarrassed. "I came home to change my shirt. I was so mad at Gerald I'd slammed my hand against the wall and got blood all over myself. Then I went out and took a look at Gary's stuff. I found Gary's ID in his spare boots, but then I lost it somewhere."

That explained his bruised hand I'd wondered about that first night at dinner. I didn't tell him I'd found Gary's ID and I hoped Katy wouldn't remember.

"Why didn't you call me right then?" Cato asked. His expression was mild enough, but it didn't take a rocket scientist to tell he was angry. A lot of grief might have been avoided if Billy Joe had done that.

"I did," Billy Joe protested. "I called before I even left the airport. You were in El Paso and weren't due back until Thursday. So I called Arnold Johnson and told him the whole story. He told me to send Gerald in to his office right then, which I did, and not to say a word to anyone else, that he'd take care of contacting you. When you showed up at the club that night talking about Gary's death being an accident I figured he'd told you all about it and that was how you wanted to play it."

"I came back early for another reason entirely, and I didn't hear from Arnold until late the following day," Cato said. He turned to frown at me. "And why didn't you bother telling me what you'd seen?" he asked.

I nearly dropped the glass of wine Billy Joe had poured me. "I . . . uh . . . I'm not sure . . ."

"My nephew runs the service station at the edge of

town," he said severely. "He remembered washing the mica dust off a blue Toyota with a Washington license plate— *your* Toyota—at about the same time the coroner set the time of the murder. And there's only one road in the county surfaced with gravel containing mica dust."

I remembered the glittering dust swirling around the car as I fled from the gravel dump. "I was afraid," I said flatly, deciding to tell the truth. "I thought . . ." I stopped, started again, and finally told them what I'd seen and heard in the country club hall, and what I'd thought.

"Never having seen the two of you, you and Calvin, together I didn't realize you were close to the same height and from the back at least, looked much the same. It finally dawned on me when Calvin walked down the stairs in front of me the night of Velma Jean's party."

"It seems we've all made some mistakes," Cato said eventually.

"How did you know . . . ?" Billy Joe stopped and cleared his throat. "How did you guess . . . ?"

"That it was Gerald in the bag?" I helped him out.

He nodded.

"Had to be. No one else was missing and I knew, guessed, from almost the beginning that he had to be the other person in the fight. He fit, no one else did. Plus, Calvin was the last person we know of that had any contact with him. On the highway by the rest stop. Which, at least to me, suggested that he was Gerald's killer. Plus he lied to the sheriff here about the direction he was going. He said he was eastbound on the highway while Gerald told Linda Calvin was right behind him. Westbound."

Cato nodded. "Forensics has already placed Gerald in Calvin's car, so he lied about simply waving to him, but how and when he killed Gerald we don't know yet. We will." The last was in a grim tone that suggested Calvin would tell him all he wanted to know, sooner or later.

"Have you asked him about the cocaine, or whatever was in those bags?" I asked, not really expecting him to answer. To my way of thinking they had all underestimated Calvin's abilities. I said as much. "Personally, I think he killed Gerald because somehow Gerald found out he was smuggling dope. Probably found out the night someone brought the woman with her arm cut off into the hospital. Gerald was at the hospital that night. All of you seemed to think both Calvin and Gerald were a bit dim, but Calvin was sharp enough to set up a drug-running operation right under your nose."

Cato colored slightly. "Yes, he did," he said finally. "And none of us were alert enough to realize that while he wasn't smart, he was cunning, cunning enough to use his job for cover."

About that time Katy, who had gone inside to talk to Carmella, returned with Aunt Crystle, who not only acted solicitous, but was actually very pleasant and congenial. I didn't know how Katy felt about it, but I was so surprised I swallowed the rest of my wine in one gulp and went over to the table myself to refill it.

Crystle had several surprises in store for the group that evening. She had known from the beginning that Calvin had killed Gary, which accounted for a lot of her hostile behavior. She distrusted me—I was a Yankee—and was afraid I'd somehow involve Billy Joe in what she called "a sorry situation."

Billy Joe hadn't told her about the murder. His lawyer, Arnold Johnson, had. That was part of her bombshell and it nearly blew Billy Joe away.

"We tell each other everything," Crystle informed us. "That is the only way to form a lasting relationship. We are going to be married in December."

Billy Joe gaped at her. "But you're sixty years old," he said, as if that precluded thoughts of marriage.

She gave him the kind of acid glance that must have stopped him in his tracks as a teenager.

Turning to Katy and me she said, "Katy will be my matron of honor, of course. And I'll be delighted if you will be one of my attendants."

Both Katy and I nodded dumbly.

I swallowed that glass of wine at a gulp too and poured my third.

Late on that next morning I ate my last Carmella breakfast—as delicious as all the others had been—said my final goodbyes all around, hugged Katy one last time, promised to return for the wedding, and Calvin's trial if necessary, and drove out of the yard.

Two hours later I turned west on I-10 and headed for San Diego and the intersection with I-5. There are a lot of miles between Del Rio and Seattle and I was anxious to get back to the cool, green, Pacific Northwest and its moderate temperatures. Seattle might not be paradise, it did rain some, but with snow-capped mountains on one side and the sparkle of Puget Sound on the other, the scenery sure beat barb wire fencing and mesquite.

There really is no place like home.